Something Special

by BARBARA BARTHOLOMEW

G.K.HALL &CO.
Boston, Massachusetts
1984

Copyright © 1984 by Barbara Bartholomew

Published in Large Print by arrangement with
Simon & Schuster, Inc.

SILHOUETTE INSPIRATIONS is a trademark of
Simon & Schuster, Inc.

Set in 16 pt English Times

Library of Congress Cataloging in Publication Data

Bartholomew, Barbara, 1941-
  Something special.

  ''Published in large print''—T.p. verso.
  1. Large type books. I. Title.
PS3552.A7637S6 1984   813'.54   84-4525
ISBN 0-8161-3730-7
ISBN 0-8161-3696-3 (pbk)

Something Special

Chapter One

Trudy stared across the desk at the white-haired professor. "I'm a graduate student," she protested. "What kind of assignment are you giving me?"

Dr. Lorimer leaned back in his chair, his eyes twinkling. "I assure you, Miss McClung, I think carefully before making assignments to my students. Journalism isn't all political scandals and investigative reporting, you know. Here at Mansfield College we expect our students to have well-rounded training."

Trudy rose to her feet, the high heels she'd worn to give added height to her five-foot-one-inch frame clicking authoritatively against the floor of the classroom. She walked over to the window, hardly seeing the students clustered on the grassy slope below.

She was well aware of the reputation of her faculty adviser. Dr. Lorimer might look like a beardless Santa, but the word was that he was tough. Students who survived him emerged as first-rate newspeople. That was what she wanted.

Still this assignment didn't make sense. She turned back to face him.

"I'm not a first-year student." She tried to keep her voice calm. "I'm twenty-four years old; I have my bachelor's degree and a year of newspaper experience."

He nodded. "I'm aware of your excellent record. We don't allow just anyone to work as a graduate assistant with our students."

She stood resolutely, facing him across the desk. She didn't sit down, feeling somehow that he'd listen more seriously if she remained standing.

"Then why?" She raised her hands in a questioning gesture. "A survey of local church pastors to find out how they feel about their work? What can they say? When you've spent years working toward a goal, you aren't going to admit it might have been a mistake."

"A good interviewer can always get beneath the surface, Miss McClung," he pointed out gently, running one hand absentmindedly through his already ruffled hair.

It was hard to keep her temper under control. "But church pastors, Dr. Lorimer. I'm not a churchy person. We won't even be able to communicate."

2

Suddenly he rose to his feet and the sparkle died from his eyes. "If I were your city editor, would you question this assignment?" he asked crisply.

"Well, no, I suppose not, but . . ."

"Regard me as your editor, Miss McClung. During the year you will spend doing graduate work with us, I will be just that. Now, get busy on your assignment and see to it you do a thorough job on the research."

His unflinching glare met hers for a moment; then Trudy's gaze dropped. She had no choice. Bad assignment or not, she had to do it.

"Yes, sir." She barely managed to keep her tone polite.

She strode angrily away from the journalism building, blindly passing crowds of laughing, chatting students who lingered in the autumn afternoon long after most classes had ended.

She tried to relax. It was no good allowing herself to get so tense over every little thing, but she couldn't seem to help it. She glanced around again, observing the students nearby. They looked attractive in their deep-toned fall clothes, the girls smiling brightly at tall young men, talking about parties and clothes and the year ahead.

Trudy set her mouth grimly at the thought of what this year would mean to her. It was the same as always, the way it had been ever since her first year in high school when she'd decided that achievement and hard work were the only way out of the trap. Since then she'd had no time for fun and friendships. Those were luxuries for other girls, girls with normal homes and families. She would have to fight for everything she got, and this year at graduate school was just another step in that struggle.

A tall, blond young man stepped suddenly into her path.

"Miss McClung," he said, smiling at her with confident charm. She had little choice but to stop and stare at him with annoyance.

He looked at her as though expecting to be recognized—probably one of her students. After only a few days of classes, and considering the fact that over fifty students a day came through the little newsroom, how could she recognize all of them?

"I work on the *Daily*," he told her, speaking as though that fact should interest her.

"You're one of the editors?" She tried to remember if he'd been one of the students who'd sat around the long table at the staff meeting the previous afternoon.

He shook his head, looking only slightly deflated. "I'm in Journalism one-oh-six," he explained.

It was hard not to smile. J106 was for those newly admitted to the journalism program. To be in 106 was something like being a first-year student at West Point. You did all the dirty work, followed orders from any upper-class journalism student, and generally were the lowest of the low.

"Welcome to the journalism school, One-Oh-Six," she told him.

"I was telling my friends"—he gestured toward a small group of boys who were gathered a few feet away—"that you were the prettiest teacher in school."

So it was that kind of problem again. Trudy drew her petite body as tall as she could. She wore high heels and businesslike tailored suits to school. Her brown hair was severely drawn to the back of her head. But being small and feminine-looking was a severe disability in the academic world, and she had to make up for it by force of character.

"We'll see how pretty you think I am after I edit your first copy, One-Oh-Six."

Involuntarily he stepped back. "You already did," he confessed sheepishly. "You ripped right through it. Apparently I didn't do a thing right."

"You'll do better before you finish the course," Trudy assured him, "or I'll know the reason why."

She walked around and past him. She had no patience with students like him, young people accustomed to getting by on charm and good looks. She would see to it that the boy, whatever his name was, got a good education . . . or went into an entirely different profession.

Her routine included stopping off at the student union cafeteria for dinner after finishing classes. She tried to put the blond boy and all her other students out of her mind as she walked into the

5

low, modern building. Usually the dining room was more crowded. She supposed it was because it was Friday and many students chose to leave the campus for fancier meals.

The food was plain but good, and she was too tired to look further for something to eat. She selected a chicken pot pie, still steaming beneath its crust, a small salad, and hot tea, and then took them to a small table in the corner.

She planned to look over the day's notes while she ate. She sighed, thinking again of the unpleasant assignment Dr. Lorimer had given her. She was a serious reporter and this was not serious work.

Her annoyance increased when she realized she hadn't gotten a lemon slice for her tea. She walked back to the serving area for the forgotten item. Preoccupied with thoughts of the undesirable project to which she would have to direct her efforts, she walked past the cashier and, instead of going back around properly, entered the cafeteria line from the opposite end. A tall figure moved abruptly from around the curve in the line, bumping into her with a tray heavy with food.

Her spiky heels didn't offer much in the way of secure footing. She slipped and would have fallen except that he dropped the tray to stop her fall with strong arms that caught her halfway to the floor. Dishes clattered around her as she felt herself being righted as easily as though she were a small child. "Sorry," a deep voice sounded.

She looked up . . . and up. He was an exceptionally tall man. "That's all right," she answered shakily. "It was my fault." She tried to laugh. "I'm afraid I was going the wrong way on a one-way street."

Cafeteria attendants hurried toward them. Those in the line behind him stared. Trudy felt her face warm with embarrassment. "I'm afraid I spoiled your dinner," she apologized.

He chuckled, bending to pick up dishes and place them back on the tray. Trudy tried to help. Jell-O quivered on the floor, salad and roast beef were strangely mixed, and a hot biscuit had rolled halfway into the dining area.

She retrieved it. "I'm so sorry," she murmured in embarrassment. "Please let me purchase another meal for you."

"That's not necessary." She was conscious of a gentle amusement in his smile. She wasn't much of a help, but in record time he and the student helpers had the floor clean again.

He turned to the cashier. "I'm not quite certain how much I owe you, Mrs. Hawkins," he said, "but if you'll make an estimate, I'll gladly pay."

"I'll pay," Trudy insisted, stepping closer. "It was my fault. I'll be happy to pay."

The middle-aged cashier ignored her, smiling up at the tall man. "It was only an accident, Dr. Harper. Go back through the line and get another tray."

Trudy wasn't content to leave it that way. She'd been responsible for the embarrassing accident. She liked to pay her own way and didn't accept favors from anyone.

She pulled a bill from her purse. "Here." She tried to shove it at the man.

He took her arm instead, leading her out of the way of the line and into the dining area. "Where's your table?" he asked.

"Over there." She gestured, not understanding.

He guided her to it and saw that she was seated. "You're sure you're all right?" he asked somewhat anxiously.

It was a new feeling, being treated as if she were some kind of fragile flower. Trudy detested it.

"I'm fine," she answered stiffly. "I didn't actually fall, thanks to you. And I'm sorry I ever thought I needed lemon for my tea."

"Lemon?" He looked down at the table, then nodded. He walked away without another word, and she decided, thankfully, that she'd seen the last of him.

Thank goodness! That was so embarrassing. She simply had to focus more attention on what she was doing.

She took a sip of tea, then a bite of the chicken pie. It was still hot and good, but she wasn't very hungry. She tried to look at her notes again, but it was hard to focus her attention. She reminded herself that a good diet was important and that she couldn't afford to be ill. Taking another bite of the main dish as though going through an unpleasant routine, she read another paragraph from her notes.

"Here's your lemon." She stared at the yellow slice held on a napkin in front of her, then looked up.

Him again!

She tried to smile. "That was very thoughtful, but unnecessary."

He had a tray of food balanced with an athlete's grace on one arm. "Mind if I join you?"

She did mind. But she could hardly say so. Not when he's been so gracious about her spilling his whole tray of food—and then bringing her that lemon slice. . . .

"Please do." She indicated the chair across from her.

He put his food on the table, placed the tray in a nearby rack, then sat down. "I was concerned that you might be more shaken than you thought. Almost falling like that is sometimes worse than an actual fall. You might have strained something."

"Nothing's strained," Trudy answered, glancing wistfully at her notes. She had a lot of work to do and no time to waste chatting with a total stranger. "I'm really fine."

"You're quite a little thing to have the experience of running into a former fullback."

So he was that type. She glanced across knowingly at the rugged masculine face opposite her. Probably in his midthirties. The big moment in his life had probably been a college football game a decade and a half ago, and he probably

9

liked to go around telling people about it. She felt sorry for people like that.

"I'm fine," she assured him again firmly.

"If you say so." He still sounded doubtful.

If she had to talk to him, she might as well switch the conversation to a less personal topic than her physical well-being.

"You played football?" she asked politely, hardly caring.

"Years ago." He had the grace to look uncomfortable. "Do you like the sport?"

"Not really," she answered, then realized she'd been abrupt. She tried to make amends with a small joke. "I was always too small to make the team."

He smiled at her. "Are you a student here?"

"Graduate assistant in the journalism school." She didn't even have to ask him what he did. Doubtless he was a member of the athletic staff.

He hadn't begun his meal yet. "Excuse me," he said, bending his face toward the table for a silent moment.

She studied him curiously. He was probably into religion, though he hardly looked the type.

A second later he smiled at her again and began to eat. Interested now in the contradiction between his appearance and his behavior, she covertly observed this unexpected dinner companion.

He was unusually tall and well built, with shoulders that looked as if they were designed to sweep across a football field. His face was so strongly designed, it might have been chipped from granite. It wasn't handsome exactly, though attractive. His eyes were deep blue and looked at her kindly, and his hair was an unusually bright gold with a touch of silver shading the temples.

She realized then that she was staring and looked down quickly. But he, too, seemed to be taking her measure.

"You look very young to be a grad," he told her.

It was easy to smile at him. "That fact is getting to be the bane of my existence. I worked police beat on a big-city newspaper all last year. People kept thinking I was a kid tagging along for a thrill."

He raised expressive eyebrows. "There are worse things than being thought young for your age."

"Not if you want to teach college students only a few years younger than you."

He nodded in understanding, then ate a few bites of roast beef. "Police beat. That sounds dangerous."

She shook her head. "Mostly not. Mostly plain grinding routine. A lot of reporting is like that —research, routine, and lots of hard work."

She suddenly realized she was talking too much about herself. She didn't often do that because she'd learned a long time ago, as a child living in one foster home after another, that people asked personal questions for one of two reasons: One was just to be polite and they couldn't care less about the answers—most adults didn't actually listen to children—and the second was because they wanted to dig out information to use against you.

Suspiciously she glanced at her companion. He could have no other reason than simple politeness. It was her turn to ask the proper questions, make the right responses.

"How about you, Dr. Harper?" she asked.

His brow wrinkled. "You know my name?"

"The cashier mentioned it." She indicated the woman with a wave of one hand.

"But I don't know yours."

"It's Trudy," she told him. "Not short for Gertrude, though that was my grandmother's name. Trudy McClung."

He reached a massive hand across the table and she took it, finding her own small fingers lost in his. "Jeremy Harper," he told her in an elaborate drawl. "Pleased to make your acquaintance, ma'am."

She laughed. "I suppose you're on staff here?" she asked, feeling sure of the answer.

But he shook his head. "Just a student. I'm taking a philosophy course. An evening class." He glanced at his watch. "I still have a few minutes before it begins."

She was grateful for the time. It was funny, considering how reluctant she'd been to have him join her, but it was lonely always eating alone.

"Philosophy . . ." She dared speak her thought aloud. "I wouldn't have thought it

12

would interest you."

He grinned like a small boy. "You figured I wouldn't like to make my head hurt thinking about the whys and wherefores of existence?"

"Most people don't. You look like a no-nonsense man to me."

His expression turned suddenly serious. "I was that way once," he admitted, "but I've gotten fascinated with the human animal and its thinking process, I guess . . . it's difficult to explain."

Trudy nodded thoughtfully. "I try not to think too much about people. Sometimes I'd like to go hide in a cave all by myself. People are cruel and uncaring."

"Journalism, newspapers," he mused, studying her as though sizing up her character. "That's not what I'd call hiding away from society."

She tried to smile, tried to make light of it. It was no good trusting your feelings to strangers. "I don't make judgments. I only report events."

"But what made you choose this field?"

"Beginnings are a struggle, but there are lots of places to go. I'm good at what I do and I'm ambitious. Very ambitious."

She glanced around at the nearly deserted dining room. Here she was, confessing the most secret desires of her heart to a virtual stranger. What was it about this man that seemed to lead her to confide in him? She had to be careful. In a minute she'd break down and sob to him about her miserable past, about her mother, and about other girls' pretty clothes and how rotten it was to grow up alone.

"Nothing wrong with a little ambition," he told her. "Properly directed, of course. We're expected to use our talents, not bury them in the ground."

She stared openly at him, trying to keep from laughing at a mental picture of herself digging a hole to bury her typewriter.

She led the talk in other directions and discovered a mutual interest in classical music, old movies, and the outdoors.

"I hope to get a cabin at one of the state parks for at least one weekend while I'm here," she told him. "I like to get away and hear birds sing and water ripple and all that."

She didn't tell him that such experiences had been rare in her life, that only once, back in seventh grade, she'd lived with a family with an enthusiasm for camping.

"I always work weekends," he told her, "but if you have time during the week, there's a nice state park about an hour from here. We could drive over and have a picnic."

"That would be fun," she agreed enthusiastically, then inched back a little further in her chair, wondering if she'd lost her mind. Friendships were made easily on any college campus, she knew that. There was rarely anyone around to provide introductions, but she wasn't about to go off in a car somewhere with a stranger.

"You sound as though you're new to this part of the state," he continued, not seeming to notice her withdrawal. "Didn't you do your under-graduate work here?"

She shook her head. "I went to the university the first four years, worked last year, and then was accepted as a graduate assistant here."

"Mansfield's a good school."

They were both talking, Trudy suddenly realized, just to keep the conversation going. They didn't know enough about each other to know what to say, but he didn't want to leave. She didn't want him to leave.

Silence fell on the table. Trudy glanced down at her own virtually empty plate. His dinner was finished too, so there was no excuse to linger.

"You'll be late for your class," she reminded him, not looking up.

He didn't say anything for a moment. "Do you eat here often?" he asked abruptly.

She looked up. "Nearly every evening. Just about the same time." She heard the eagerness in her own voice.

"I'll see you again then." His smile warmed her one final time; then he was gone in long strides that carried him quickly from her sight.

I'll see you again then. That was what he'd said. Her elation faded rapidly. It had sounded different when he had said it. But now that she repeated the words in her own mind she realized they were conventional, just one of those things people said.

She slowly gathered her belongings together, and strolled the few blocks to the rooming house

15

where she lived.

The house, once a comfortable single-family residence but now divided into rooms for students, was deserted, unlit except for the front hall. Trudy found her way upstairs and into her own room, a large one in front with twin beds covered with identical yellow chenille spreads.

This was the one luxury she allowed herself. After many years of sharing rooms, first in foster homes and institutions, then in college dormitories, it was heavenly just to have a room of her own.

She put books and papers down on her desk, then went to look out the window at the street below. Friday night and everyone else in the house was out having a good time. Even Mr. and Mrs. Larson, the owners, were visiting friends.

She tried not to feel envious. Someday she would have time for friends . . . maybe even a family. But there was so much to do first!

She shook off her longings as she took a quick bath, then settled herself against a couple of pillows in bed, prepared for hours of reading. But her mind wouldn't settle easily to its appointed task. Instead she found herself thinking of Jeremy Harper. He seemed like someone who would be nice to know.

Not a romance, of course. She didn't have time for that, not for a while yet. But he could be a good friend, someone to talk to, someone who would share experiences with her.

She remembered the year before last when she'd

graduated with honors at the big state university and there had been no one in that huge crowd to be proud of her. And last year she had won a prize for a feature she'd written and there had been no one to tell but her co-workers.

My friend, Jeremy. Meet my friend, Jerry Harper. He looked like a Jerry, sweet and kind. She hoped he would stop by the cafeteria again looking for her.

But then she frowned. You couldn't judge people by the way they looked. She remembered one of the foster homes where the woman looked like a chubby, cuddly, motherly type, with a lap made for children. But when the social worker left, she'd screamed foul language and told Trudy to get out of her sight.

No telling what Jeremy Harper was really like. She'd change the time when she stopped by the cafeteria so as to be sure to avoid any future encounters with him.

Resolutely she forced her mind to concentrate on the day's work, on grading the editorials from editing class and considering how to approach the deadly assignment Dr. Lorimer had given her.

The grading was easy enough. Most of the work was decidedly inferior, with only one or two shining exceptions. But the assignment was another matter.

How could Dr. Lorimer give her such a boring, meaningless assignment?

The thing to do was to get on the phone tomorrow and start lining up appointments. She fell asleep, thinking of the questions she would ask.

Only vaguely were her dreams troubled by the sound of the other residents coming late into the house, their smothered laughter and happy good-nights echoing down the halls.

But she awakened the next morning with a sense of dissatisfaction. It wasn't fair. Everyone else seemed to be getting more out of life than she was.

Trudy felt impatient with herself. The only way to get out of this mood was to dive right into her work. She started making calls before breakfast. The calls were largely fruitless. Nobody answered at the majority of the churches.

She considered the problem over scrambled eggs and toast at a campus corner diner.

"Must be nice being in church work," she muttered to herself. "Short hours."

"Beg pardon?" The waitress looked at her questioningly.

"Never mind." Trudy shook her head. "I was only talking to myself. I've been trying to get hold of some of the local pastors, only nobody seems to be at home."

"At home?" The little waitress looked confused.

"I mean no one answers at the churches, at least not at most of them."

"Course not. It's Saturday morning. But if you've got a problem, I can give you the home phone number of the pastor at my church. He's a great guy and will be glad to listen to anything."

"No, that's not it," Trudy tried to explain, uncomfortable at the idea that she might be looking for someone in whom to confide.

"You can tell him anything." The girl touched Trudy's sleeve earnestly. "He's popular with the students. Many of them go to his church because he has a way with young people."

Trudy tried not to grimace. She could well imagine what a pastor would be like who had a "way" with young people.

"I'll simply attend Sunday morning services," she decided. "That'll be the best way to get started."

"Go to the McFarlin Street Church." The girl pointed down the street. "Just turn off Elm."

Later, Trudy continued her calls and managed to set up some appointments for the next week, but for the sake of the waitress, she tried several times to reach the McFarlin Street Church. Nobody answered. Must be nice to work only on Sundays.

She'd make it a point to visit there first.

She allowed herself a brief walk during her usual dinner hour, going to the student center an hour late to eat alone, a book in front of her.

She studied late, and when the alarm went off the next morning, she stirred reluctantly, tempted to turn it off. But the thought of Dr. Lorimer was enough to get her out of bed.

She showered hastily and allowed herself the luxury of wearing a soft lilac-colored summer dress. Might as well. Fall would be hitting in earnest soon, and it would be too cold for such a lightweight dress.

She walked the few blocks to the church, pausing uncertainly outside the white stone building. She had a premonition that she should turn and walk hurriedly away, that going in here could change her whole life.

How foolish.

She walked inside and was shown into the crowded auditorium by a gray-haired usher. The service was already under way, and the people were standing singing something about a sweet holy spirit.

Trudy found herself placed next to a couple of impish-faced boys who looked anything but devout. She grinned down at them. It was only when the song ended that she looked toward the front.

The minister was coming into the pulpit. "Please be seated," he said.

Trudy gasped audibly. It was the man from the cafeteria. It was Jeremy Harper.

The little boy next to her kicked her leg. "You're supposed to sit down," he whispered loudly.

Chapter Two

As soon as the service ended, Trudy slipped quickly out the back and into the hall. Dr. Lorimer would have to do without the name of one leading local minister in his assigned article. She would refuse to interview Jeremy Harper.

He had deceived her. He had masqueraded as an ordinary person that night in the student cafeteria. She tried to think what she'd told him, if she'd said anything that shouldn't be spoken in front of a clergyman.

Her attempt to escape without meeting him again failed. He was waiting at the exit, smiling and shaking hands as people departed. She turned to look for another way out, but he saw her, his eyes widening in surprise.

"Trudy McClung," he said, taking her hand in his and sounding pleased. Trudy looked around anxiously. What would his church people think? "I'm so glad you came."

"I didn't know," Trudy tried to explain. "I mean it was only part of my work. . . ."

He smiled. "You mean if you'd known who was preaching, you wouldn't have dropped in today."

That was exactly what she'd meant. But she wasn't about to admit it. "It was a lovely sermon," she told him, even though she'd hardly heard a word he'd said. The rest of the congregation had seemed interested enough, but she'd been too surprised by his mere presence up in front of the church to concentrate on words.

But she was in the way. People were waiting to shake hands with their pastor. She tried to withdraw her hand. Slowly he released it.

"Wait," he said. "I want to talk to you."

Well, Dr. Lorimer wanted her to talk to him too, but she wasn't going to wait around just to please them. She hurried out of the church and down the steps.

One of the two small boys who'd sat next to her in church met her there. "Hi," he said.

"Hello," she returned the greeting doubtfully. She hadn't had much experience dealing with children since her own childhood. She spoke to him as she might have to an adult. "Did you enjoy the church service?"

He shrugged. "I liked that one song where the lady's voice got too high and screeched a little."

Trudy looked around hastily. She had a view of

church people as being solemn and humorless. She was sure they wouldn't like such a critical view of one of their soloists.

"It was pretty bad," she admitted cautiously.

"That was Melissa Reven. She wants to marry Jerry."

Jerry. She'd guessed he'd be called that.

She frowned at the little boy. With his blond hair and huge eyes, he had an angelic appearance hardly matched by his disposition. She allowed the frown to melt into a smile. Angel children must be dull.

"Jerry?" she asked, certain already of the answer. "You mean Dr. Harper?"

"Sure." He stuck his hands into the pockets of his Sunday dress pants. "Though nobody calls him that much. Mostly they say Jerry or Jeremy or Brother Harper. I say Jerry because he's known me for a long time, ever since I was born."

Quite a number of people had left the church by now and were clustered in front of the building. Trudy decided she dared not wait any longer. Jeremy Harper might come out any minute, and she didn't want to talk to him. She didn't know what to say to a preacher!

"I have to go now." She smiled at her new friend. "It was nice talking to you."

He nodded as though accustomed to the effect of his devastating charm on the opposite sex. "You walking?"

She nodded. "I live near here." She started out

23

and he hopped along on one foot at her side.

"I'll walk with you," he offered.

"But won't your mother be worried?"

He shook his head. "Nope. She knows I'm practically grown up. Anyway, I came with my brother and he'll be glad to get rid of me."

"If you're sure your family won't mind." She hesitated, not sure what her responsibilities were.

"I walk all the time," he assured her.

He strode along importantly at her side. "What's your name?" he asked.

"Trudy McClung."

"I'm Philip Granbury," he informed her, "but I like to be called Phil."

"Pleased to meet you, Phil."

They walked. Or rather, Trudy walked while Phil ran, jumped, skipped, and paused to dangle from the low-hanging limb of an oak. Under the circumstances, little conversation was required.

Trudy thought how nice it would be if adults were such easy companions. She recalled the brief dinner with Jeremy Harper. It wasn't fair. Clergymen should always wear black like a priest, or something special, something that announced their calling, so people didn't go around making idiots of themselves thinking they were football players. Of course, he'd only said he *had* been a football player. She shook her head crossly, trying to piece together the ill-fitting puzzle that made up Jeremy . . . Dr. Harper, she corrected herself mentally.

"What are you so mad about?" Phil was once more at her side, looking up at her curiously.

"Not mad," she answered automatically. There was no point in being less than truthful to this child she hardly knew. "Only disappointed. Someone turned out to be different than I thought."

"Like you thought he was a nice guy and he turned out to be a crook?"

She couldn't help smiling. "Not exactly. Just different, that's all."

He swung off on another far-ranging detour. He must cover double the amount of territory of any grown-up, she thought.

She was reluctant to say good-bye when they reached the front of the building where she was making her home, but he waved and she went inside. The meeting with the little boy had cheered an otherwise dismal morning.

She decided she wouldn't bother with lunch, but would work right through the afternoon. She was deep in a massive textbook when, at about two o'clock, the phone rang. She scowled at it, then answered impatiently.

She recognized the voice of the caller at once. It was Jeremy Harper.

"You got away so quickly this morning that we didn't get a chance to talk." There was a slight note of scolding in his voice, as though he realized the quick escape had been deliberate.

"I had to get home. I have work to do."

"But I told you to wait," he reminded her.

"I don't always do as I'm told." She kept her tone light even though she was angered by his

25

attitude. Then she reminded herself of his position. This was no way to talk to a minister. Even if she was not a churchgoer, she owed respect to his profession. "I'm sorry, Dr. Harper." She moderated her tone to what she hoped was a serious, appropriately formal level. "But I was anxious to get back to my work."

"Don't you ever take time off? Even that night in the cafeteria I noticed you had a stack of books with you."

"Normally I read while I eat." She kept her voice at the same polite but distant level. "It saves time."

"Saves time for what?"

She didn't quite know how to respond to the blunt question. "Saves time so I can work some more, I suppose," she answered, hearing the tiniest trickle of irritation enter into her voice. Church pastor or not, it would be easy to be annoyed with his take-charge manner.

He didn't comment further on the subject. "I wanted to talk to you anyway, but I do have a special reason for calling."

She frowned at the receiver. "What's that?"

"You were seen walking away from the church with a small blond boy."

What was this? Did he have spies watching her every move?

"How did you get my telephone number?" she questioned sharply. "It's not in the book."

"I called information," he explained reasonably. "I told them it would probably be a new listing because you'd said you just moved here."

"Oh." She should have gotten an unlisted number.

"Did you see that little boy?" he asked sharply. Something in his voice made her suddenly aware it was something more than a casual question.

"Has something happened to Phil?" she asked anxiously.

"You did see him." His voice was relieved.

"He walked me to my door, and I thought he was going right on home. He assured me his older brother would approve."

"Phil is my nephew and he lives five miles out of town," Dr. Harper told her in a quiet voice. "And his big brother, though not always the most responsible nineteen-year-old in the world, is most concerned about what has happened to him. In fact, the whole family is worried."

Trudy took in the information silently. "He seemed such a little boy," she volunteered fearfully. "He can't be very old."

"He's seven, going on seventeen." Jeremy didn't sound all that worried. "And has a slight talent for trouble."

"Yes." Trudy remembered the delightful dancing eyes that had looked up at her in church. "I could see that."

"It's been a while since you saw him?"

"At least a couple of hours. He was going off down the street to the south when I came inside. He acted as though he knew exactly where he was going."

27

"The south." He registered the information. "Thanks, that might help."

"Should I go out and look for him?" Trudy asked impulsively. "He might be playing somewhere in this neighborhood."

"I'll be right over," he answered, "and we can look together." She heard the phone click decisively. "Wait!" she called futilely into the phone. "You don't know where I live."

It was no use; he was already gone. She sighed. No doubt the information operator had given him her address as well.

She'd have to go through with it. Quickly she slipped off the lightweight robe she'd been wearing to study and reached for jeans and a plaid shirt. She held them, studying them doubtfully for a moment.

Jeans and a shirt. Probably inappropriate garments to wear in the company of a minister, even on an emergency child-hunting expedition. She put them back in the closet and took out a somber gray skirt and a plain white blouse.

Once dressed, she recombed her hair and fastened it back in its usual severe arrangement. The whole process hardly took more than five minutes, and she was waiting on the front porch when a small, dark green sports car pulled up to the curb.

She had to look twice because, of course, Dr. Jeremy Harper wouldn't be driving such a car. Only he was.

"Let's go." He indicated the seat beside him

and she climbed in, still stunned by yet another piece that didn't fit into the puzzle.

They cruised slowly down the street. When she saw a little group of playing children, Trudy's heart quickened its beat. She touched his arm, and he pulled over so they could ask questions. But the two girls they spoke to denied any knowledge of Phil.

"We wouldn't play with a *little* boy," a pretty freckle-faced girl explained scornfully from the vantage point of a mature nine-year-old.

They drove on.

"You're not seriously concerned about him, are you?" Trudy questioned, frowning. "I mean, you're not thinking in terms of an accident . . . or a kidnapping. Not in a small town like this, Dr. Harper."

"Jeremy," he corrected in an abstracted voice.

"What did you say?" Startled, she turned to him.

"Call me Jeremy."

Jeremy. She couldn't do that. It wouldn't seem right. She set her mouth grimly. It would make them sound like friends, and they weren't; she couldn't be friends with him.

"I asked if you were seriously worried about your nephew, Dr. Harper," she told him, placing only a delicate emphasis on the title.

They cruised slowly down the tree-lined streets of the old college town. The leaves were beginning to turn as fall made its colorful entrance, and the crispness of the air belied the summery look of the afternoon.

It was more than a moment before he answered. "Phil doesn't mean to get into trouble, but somehow he always does. He's a bright youngster, but I'm afraid my sister has spoiled him a little. He's much younger than his brother."

Trudy couldn't have cared less about Phil's brother. "You didn't answer my question," she reminded him.

"I'm only saying that Phil is perfectly capable of getting himself into trouble."

He didn't have to say more. Trudy could well imagine some of the situations an overly adventurous seven-year-old might get into. She scanned yards and alleys with intense scrutiny.

"What about his friend?" she asked suddenly. "They didn't leave church together, but they might have met later. He could even have gone to the other boy's home."

"Friend?" His forehead wrinkled into a frown.

"A boy who looked to be a little older, maybe eight or nine. Brown hair, brown eyes." She hesitated over the last part of the description. "Clothes looked a little shabby, at least compared to the way Phil was dressed."

For the first time since she'd gotten into the car, she became aware of what Jeremy Harper was wearing. He was dressed in well-worn jeans and a casual shirt. And after she'd gone to the trouble of dressing up for his benefit!

He sure didn't know much about being a clergyman.

He shook his head thoughtfully, obviously considering her description. "I can't think of anyone like that. We have a small church. I'm well acquainted with most of the members."

"Small!" Trudy protested. "There must have been over four hundred people there today. How can you know all of them?"

He didn't argue. "How could I have missed seeing this boy when everyone was leaving? I stood right at the door."

She shrugged. "Easy enough for a child to slip out from among a crowd of adults. Maybe he didn't want to shake your hand."

"That's possible." He grinned. Suddenly he snapped his fingers. "Mike Taylor," he said.

"You know him?"

He shook his head. "Never met him. But my sister's been complaining to me about a new friend Phil has. Said he lives in that run-down area over west of the college. She didn't think he was a good influence on Phil."

Trudy raised both eyebrows expressively. "You mean he's poor?"

Jeremy hesitated, and she decided she'd hit the nail directly on the head. She knew what it was like to be treated like you weren't smart enough or good enough for other kids because you didn't dress right or live in the good part of town.

"We'll drive over to that area," he told her.

Within only a few blocks, the character of the

streets began to change. Houses shrank to ill-kept frame dwellings, the aging sidewalks were badly cracked, and automobiles were parked across bare, grassless yards.

Just ahead Trudy saw a fat black puppy waddle toward the street. "Be careful." She clutched at Dr. Harper's arm, afraid the sports car would strike it.

But, in a flash, she saw that danger also came from the other direction. A red car was moving rapidly from the opposite direction toward them . . . and towards the puppy.

Suddenly the little animal became aware of the danger and, panicking, ran directly into the pathway of the onrushing automobile.

"Phil!"

She heard Jeremy's alarmed cry and then saw what he'd already observed: a small blond boy chasing after the puppy. She could see his lips moving as he shouted to the puppy to stop, but couldn't hear the sound through the closed car windows.

The red car squealed and skidded as the speeding driver fought to bring the car to a stop. But there wasn't enough room, and Trudy watched in horror as the small figure of the boy was scooped up against the shiny chrome of the front bumper, then tossed against the red hood to fall limply to the street below.

She watched a small black puppy race to safety on the other side of the street.

It seemed to take forever for Jeremy to park the

car at the side of the street. She watched the tall man leave her side and lope to the aid of the boy. As a reporter, she had seen scenes of violence many times before. But this was different. This was the little charmer who had walked her home from church only this morning.

She closed her eyes, trying to find strength, but none would come. Life was so ugly, so horrible. There was nothing else to do but face it. She got out of the car and walked shakily to where Harper was bending over a small figure.

She didn't want to see. She was afraid.

The first thing she heard was the whimpered murmurings of the young driver who'd hit the child. "I didn't see him. He just ran out. I didn't see him until it was too late. I tried to stop."

The little boy lay on his back in the middle of the street. Jeremy Harper was checking his injuries, touching him reassuringly.

He must be alive. Surely he was alive. Just then the boy's long lashes lifted, and his wide blue eyes stared past Harper and up at her.

"It's all right," his uncle soothed. "It'll be fine, Phil." He looked up at Trudy and snapped out orders. "Run and call an ambulance."

The little boy still looked around, his eyes searching, and Trudy couldn't help hesitating before following the instructions. She was frozen, barely conscious of the continued murmuring of the driver. Then her brain cleared.

"The puppy got away," she told the boy. "Not a scratch."

Phil's face, drained of color, managed to stretch into a grin.

Harper reached out to touch her hand. "Good girl," he said. "I didn't know what was bothering him. Now run!"

She ran. But house after house on the dingy little street seemed empty of life. Either that, or people just didn't bother to answer, she decided bitterly. Puffing, she ran up to the fifth house, where an elderly woman in a faded wrapper let her in and led the way to the telephone.

Moments later she heard the scream of emergency vehicles coming up the street.

"Uncle Jerry, come with me," the child pleaded as he was lifted carefully into the ambulance.

The big man nodded. "Key's still in the car," he told Trudy. "Meet me at the hospital."

She nodded. This was no time to argue, even though she didn't know where the hospital was. The police officers who had arrived to investigate the accident gave her directions, and soon she pulled the dark green sports car up in front of a new-looking brick building.

She went in through the emergency entrance. Jeremy Harper was on the phone, talking earnestly into the receiver. His face was white and drawn. She dreaded hearing what he had to tell her.

Finally he put the receiver down and came to her.

"Phil?" she asked.

"No word yet, but he was talking in the

ambulance on the way over about how he wants a puppy like that little black one. That's a good sign that nothing too bad is wrong.''

She hoped so, but she was afraid Harper was only trying to cheer her up. That was the role of a minister, wasn't it, to make people feel better by reciting comforting platitudes?

''I suppose you've got all the answers,'' she spoke bitterly.

''Answers?'' He sank wearily onto a small sofa in the tiny waiting room. ''What do you mean?''

''About why things like this happen.'' She sat down beside him, too drained to be particular over where she located herself.

He leaned back. ''It happened because Phil was so anxious about that puppy he ran right in front of a car. He's crazy about animals, just like most kids.''

''That's not what I meant!''

His eyes opened, and he looked at her thoughtfully. ''Yeah, I do know what you mean. You're wondering if just now, when I had to call Phil's mom and his stepdad, I was able to give them some wonderful lecture about the meaning of it all and the good that can come from this.''

Her anger subsided. She touched his arm. ''It must have been hard telling them.''

He nodded. ''Especially when I don't know anything yet. But they're driving right in from the country and should be here in a few minutes. His brother is still out combing the streets for him. Nobody knows how to get hold of poor Steven.''

It was awful. But Trudy tried to remind herself that it had nothing to do with her. She'd learned a long time ago that there was a tremendous amount of pain in the world and she couldn't take it all on her own shoulders. Yesterday at this time she hadn't even known Phil.

"You asked if I had any answers." His voice was intense. "I don't. But I know that nothing happens senselessly, without purpose. . . ."

"This was senseless!" she cried. "A pointless, senseless accident."

"We have to believe there's more to life than that."

Trudy looked up and saw an anxious-looking couple, the woman with blond hair like Phil's, rushing down the hall toward them. The last thing she wanted to do was to involve herself with the suffering of the little boy's parents.

"I need to leave," she said, and rushed down the hall past the unseeing couple. She turned only once to look back, saw that Jeremy's eyes were following her flight, then saw the woman grab his arm and knew he wouldn't be able to follow her.

She ran past the green sports car. She was only about a dozen blocks from home. A car had been one of the luxuries she couldn't afford. Not if she wanted to attend graduate school. But she could walk almost anyplace in this little town.

She was nearly to her rooming house when she saw a familiar face ahead. It took her a moment to place the young blond man. Oh yes, he was one of her students, the one who'd stopped her for a chat the other day.

She certainly didn't feel like a chat today. Maybe if she walked right past him . . .

His forehead was wrinkled in a frown, and at first he didn't seem to see her. He looked up and down the street before his eyes finally lighted on her.

"Hi, Miss McClung," he said, his voice dejected.

"Hi, One-Oh-Six." She managed a smile.

"Uncle Jerry said you were at church this morning, Miss McClung," the boy said. "And that my little brother walked away with you. I'd heard you lived down this way somewhere."

He continued on, but she didn't register the words. The blond student, One-Oh-Six was Jeremy Harper's other nephew. He was Steven, Phil's brother, and he didn't know about the accident. She would have to tell him!

Chapter Three

Trudy hardly knew this boy, and yet her emotions trembled at the thought of breaking the news to him. She had to make sure first.

"You're Steven Granbury?" The way she said it was like an accusation.

He nodded, looking puzzled.

"Dr. Harper's your uncle? Phil is your little brother?"

Once again he nodded, his expression confused and a little worried.

"You've heard something about Phil?" he asked. The conversation seemed to Trudy to be made up entirely of questions. She could no longer doubt that he was Phil's brother, so she had to tell him. But she couldn't dump the information on him as though burying him under a load of sand.

She tried to smile. "Let's sit down over there" —she pointed to a grassy lawn nearby—"and chat for a minute."

"Miss McClung, you're acting funny." He didn't even look in the direction indicated.

Trudy expended her breath in a long sigh. Trying to be tactful never worked for her. Sometimes it was best to come right out and say what you had to say.

"Your little brother did walk home from church with me, Steven. Then he went on, apparently looking for a friend. Your uncle became concerned about him."

"I know that," he responded impatiently. "I'm the one who told Uncle Jerry I couldn't find Phil."

"He came to me and we went looking together. We came upon him just as . . ." Vivid pictures flashed through Trudy's brain—sound, noise, color, a jumble of feelings, and a small boy stretched out on the street. "He was in an accident, Steven." It finally had to come down to honest bluntness. "Phil was hit by a car and has been taken to the hospital."

It was painful to watch his reaction. At first his eyes flickered disbelief; he wanted to say it wasn't true. "How bad?" he asked.

"I don't know. Your family was waiting to see the doctor when I left. It's only a few blocks to the hospital," she said, seizing his arm firmly. "We'll get right over there and find out what's going on. Perhaps the doctor only found a few bruises and scrapes.''

The tall young man, so much larger than herself, tried to smile. ''I hope so.''

''Then let's go!'' It was only when they were nearby to the hospital, jogging down the sidewalk, that Trudy came to her senses. A dark red leaf blew toward her and she caught it in one hand, slowing to a walk. What was she doing? She didn't want to be involved. If anything was really wrong with Phil, she'd hear about it eventually. But to go in that hospital right now, to stand with Steven and his family while they were told the news . . .

''What's wrong?'' Steven looked down at her in sudden alarm.

Trudy tried to smile. His eyes narrowed with concern, as though fearing she was keeping something from him. He might be nineteen, she thought, but he was only a boy.

''Nothing's wrong.'' She smiled, then bent to slip her fingers into the back of her shoe. ''A pebble is rubbing against my heel, that's all.'' She fished around for a moment as though something really was in the shoe, giving herself time to make a decision. Then she stood up. ''I got it out,'' she said. ''Come on, let's run.''

The decision was made as easily as that because she knew she couldn't leave this boy to face the last block and the confrontation at the hospital alone. He wasn't like her. He hadn't been brought up tough, and he wouldn't know how to take whatever was waiting for him there.

"Phil's a tough little guy." It was almost as though he had caught the word from her mind. "He could survive anything."

She didn't argue, didn't tell him that all little boys were made of flesh and blood and not designed to collide with automobiles. She knew he was talking to reassure himself.

"He'll be fine," she echoed, wishing she could believe it.

They brushed through hospital corridors at a stiff pace as Trudy led him back to the small waiting room where she had left Jeremy Harper and the couple she'd assumed to be his sister and her husband. The room was empty.

A woman dressed in white rushed past. "Nurse," Trudy called. "What happened to the people who were waiting here?" Cold dread iced her heart. Maybe it had already ended.

"People?" The nurse stared impatiently, glancing down the hall as though needing to continue with urgent work.

Trudy reminded herself that she was an experienced news reporter, accustomed to gathering information from reluctant sources. The first step was to express herself clearly. "I was waiting here with Dr. Jeremy Harper to hear news of his nephew, who'd been injured in an accident. I stepped out . . ." She glanced at Steven. "Now that I've come back, I find that Dr. Harper and his family have left."

"Dr. Harper!" The nurse smiled suddenly. "You wouldn't believe the good he does here

41

visiting the sick, especially the old and the little ones.''

"He's my uncle.'' Steven stepped forward, obviously unable to remain quiet a minute longer. "It's my little brother who's been hurt, and I was supposed to be looking after him.''

The nurse looked from Trudy to Steven. "Oh yes,'' she said, "the little blond boy.'' She seemed to hesitate. "I'm sure his doctor can tell you.''

"Just tell us where the family is,'' Trudy insisted, allowing the authority she used in dealing with her students to edge her voice. "I'm sure they can inform us as to what's going on.''

The nurse pointed to the right, around a bend in the long hall. "The little boy's been taken to surgery. The family is in the surgical waiting room.''

"Surgery!'' Steven exploded anxiously, then turned to Trudy. "That must mean he's hurt badly!''

"Not necessarily,'' Trudy assured him, patting his arm in an attempt at comfort, although she didn't know what minor injuries could have sent Phil into immediate surgery. "Let's get down there and find out before we jump to any conclusions.''

"I do hope the little boy is going to be all right,'' the nurse called after them as they hurried down the hall. "I was in emergency when he was brought in, and he looked so sweet.''

Steven raised an eyebrow in disbelief. "Sweet!'' Trudy was relieved that Steven was able to joke.

"I never heard anybody use that word to describe my brother before."

"He does look sweet with those big eyes and that golden hair," Trudy told him. A picture of the way the child had looked when she last saw him flashed into her mind; his face had been streaked with blood.

They almost went by the waiting room, but Jeremy Harper's voice stopped them. "Trudy," he called. Then he saw his nephew. "You've found Steven."

The tall figure of Dr. Harper dominated the waiting room, and though Trudy was vaguely conscious of other people behind him, at first she only registered his presence.

"Almost by accident," she replied. "He was out looking for Phil and had heard he left the church with me."

"She told me about the accident," the boy told his uncle. "How is Phil?"

"Steven!" A slender blond woman emerged from the room to throw her arms around the boy, weeping hysterically. "Thank God, you're here."

"Mom." The boy drew back impatiently. "How is Phil?"

She seemed unable to answer coherently, but an older man with graying hair came forward to slip an arm around her. "Now, Betsy," he soothed. "Let's take a little stroll while Jerry explains things to Steven and his friend."

The two of them walked slowly down the hospital corridor, the woman sobbing into the man's coat sleeve while Trudy stared after them. Steven's friend!

Harper didn't seem to notice that his sister had identified the twenty-four-year-old teacher as being with his still-teenaged nephew. "Phil is in surgery now," he said. "There's some internal bleeding. The doctor suspects the spleen is involved . . . and some broken bones. We don't know much yet because they rushed him into surgery without talking to us at length."

At last she had a decent explanation of what was known about the little boy's condition. Yet so many unanswered questions still remained. Trudy slipped past the two men and sank down on the sofa in the waiting room. Her legs had suddenly become too wobbly to support her.

This was what happened when she let herself care about people. She'd learned that painful lesson long ago. As soon as her legs returned to normal, she would get up and leave. She wouldn't let her feelings get involved in the welfare of strangers.

Jeremy Harper came over to sit down on one side of her. Steven Granbury took the seat on the other side. Jeremy took her hand. "It was good of you to go looking for Steven."

Trudy didn't like to claim undue credit. "It just happened." She moved to the edge of the sofa, preparing to stand. "I'd better go now that I know everything's being taken care of."

But before she could get to her feet, she looked up to see a woman dressed in a pale green surgical suit standing in the doorway, a face mask of the same color hanging about her neck. She looked at Dr. Harper. "Dr. Jerry," she said. "The doctor wants you to know we ran into a little problem. We had to remove the spleen, but apparently the trauma from the accident and the surgery . . ."

The woman hesitated, and Trudy could hear the thud of her own heart. Nobody said anything. Trudy felt Jeremy Harper's hand grasp her own. She squeezed, offering the only kind of assurance possible.

"His heart stopped," the woman went on. Trudy didn't know if she was a nurse, a doctor, or what. It didn't matter. "It was only for a very brief time, seconds really, but we had to take emergency action. He's all right now and the doctor is closing. We'll be moving him into recovery very shortly."

Trudy looked at Jeremy Harper. His face was drained of color. "You said his heart stopped for only seconds?"

"A very short time," she assured him again. "The chance of brain damage is . . . well, he should be fine."

The big man nodded his understanding, but Trudy could see the haunted look in his eyes, and his hand gripped hers until it was numb.

"But it shouldn't have happened," Steven spoke suddenly. "Just surgery—nothing so bad— how could something like this happen? He could have died!" In spite of the low tone, Trudy guessed the boy was close to hysteria.

45

"It's all right, Steven." Harper released her hand to go to his nephew's aid. "It's over now. He'll be all right."

Trudy also tried to comfort the boy. She put one hand on his back and patted him as though he were as young as Phil.

"It could happen again! How do you know his heart won't stop any minute now? Is someone watching him? Will they keep watching him?" Steven demanded, advancing on the woman who had brought the news.

She stepped back instinctively, nearly colliding with Betsy Granbury and her husband. The blond woman still had the protective arm of her husband around her. She looked from the distraught face of her son to the concerned features of her brother. "What's wrong?" she demanded, her voice suddenly shrill. "What's wrong with Phil?"

The woman in green took one look at her, then spoke hurriedly. "I'm sure you can handle this much better than I, Dr. Harper," she said. "It's more in your line." Then she rushed down the corridor.

Betsy Granbury shook free of her husband, grabbing her brother's hand. "Tell me." Her voice was a sobbing whisper.

"He's all right, Bets," her brother told her, his voice deep and reassuring. Trudy had only a moment to wonder at his calm in the midst of the storm of emotion from his sister and her son.

Steven whirled away from them, stalking over

to stare out a window. "Sure, he's all right *now.*" His voice was hoarse.

In a few carefully chosen words, Jeremy repeated the information just given to them. His sister's beautiful eyes filled with tears and the soft lines of her mouth quivered. "Only think if we'd lost him."

Trudy sank back down on the sofa, feeling like an intruder at this family scene. Somewhere in the back of her mind, she was always the reporter, always taking notes and making observations. Betsy Granbury, her mind recorded, a lovely woman some few years older than her brother; she must be close to twenty years younger than the distinguished man who was her husband.

Jeremy had spoken of him as the boys' step-father. Odd that they had the same last name. But he seemed as concerned about Phil as his wife was.

"They think he'll be all right now, Jerry?" he asked. "It's all well past now and he'll be fine?"

"They did say that, Jerry?" his sister insisted.

It was almost as if they were compelling him with their voices and the expressions on their faces, trying to make him say everything was going to be fine now. Trudy wanted to tell them it wouldn't make any difference, that whatever was going to happen would happen, and all the well-meant reassurance in the world wouldn't make a difference.

Jeremy Harper patted his sister's outstretched hand. "Let's say a prayer, Bets," he said. "Even the best medical personnel need a little help now and then.''

Uncomfortably, Trudy watched as the others, even Steven, bent their heads. Jeremy Harper spoke a few words. She hardly grasped what they were, only the fact that his deep voice seemed to send comforting vibrations throughout the room.

After he finished, he persuaded his brother-in-law to take his wife and Steven down to the coffee shop for something hot to drink. They agreed only when he had assured them he would let them know immediately of any news he received.

Trudy stood at his side, watching the other three walk down the hall. They hovered close together as though for comfort. She supposed that it was like that having a family, a real family of the kind she'd never known. She'd always have to walk alone through the crisis points of her own life.

She turned to look up at the man at her side. He might be wearing blue jeans and a casual, well-worn shirt, but he'd just performed the role of minister perfectly, even though his own family was the one afflicted. That must make it harder, she thought. Like a surgeon operating on a member of his own family.

She had to give him the blue ribbon for this. He'd said the right things, kept his head when others panicked. He'd even said a prayer at the right moment.

But now that they were alone, a change came over him. He turned suddenly, covering the few steps back to the sofa in two strides of his long legs, then sank down as though weighted with stones. His face had been white since that moment on the street when he bent over his nephew, but now deep lines were etched into it.

"Are you all right?" she asked.

He nodded, but seemed unable to speak.

"He'll be all right," she told him, offering what comfort she could even though it might not be true. What could you do in dark moments like this but keep saying what you hoped, like a little child in the middle of the night, denying fear?

She watched him nervously as a mouse might watch a cat, wondering if he was praying again. People who prayed this much made her uncomfortable.

"I'd better go," she said, backing toward the door.

He looked up. "Not yet," he said. "Stay with me a little."

She wanted to leave, but it was hard to resist the plea in his blue eyes. He wasn't quite so strong and sure of himself now that the others were gone. He'd given them his strength, but now there was no one he could turn to.

He touched the cushion at his side. "Sit down and talk to me."

Rather stiffly, she moved to his side. "What shall I talk about?" she asked politely. Her college training had taught her to gather information quickly and accurately, and then to present it in words. It hadn't prepared her for dealing with this kind of situation. "I don't see how I can help."

"It helps having you here." He smiled, and the corners of his eyes crinkled. "Someone pretty to tell me the world isn't such an awful place."

She wanted to help, but it was no good being less than honest. "Then you have the wrong person. I've never been accused of being an optimist."

"You're a hardheaded realist?" His tone was gently teasing, and she knew he wasn't taking her seriously. "How does a young woman just barely out of school come to have this cynicism in her soul?"

"I won't tell you the story of my life," she informed him, "but I'll listen if you want to talk."

"Afraid my biography wouldn't interest you much," he told her, the smile fading. "The trouble is that neither of us can think of much besides Phil."

She nodded somberly. Terrible visions kept circling through her brain. She had to suppress them. Maybe he was right. Maybe words were the only way. "I only met him this morning in church," she said, "but it was love at first sight."

"Phil always was a lucky boy," he assured her solemnly, but the blue eyes twinkled briefly at her. If his profession had been any other, she'd have thought he was flirting with her.

"You're the fortunate one, Dr. Harper." She tried to put the conversation back on a more appropriate basis. "You have such a loving family."

He nodded. "Betsy has tried to look after me since our parents died. She doesn't accept the idea that seven years' seniority doesn't make her my boss."

"It must be nice to have someone who cares that much." Trudy heard the wistful sound in her own voice and quickly sharpened her tone. "Though I suppose it can be a nuisance."

"Not so much these days," he assured her. "Her two boys take up most of her time, and now that she's married Miles, she's trying to play the hostess and further his career and all that. She's convinced he'll be president one of these days."

"I have heard your sister's husband mentioned politically."

"Miles served several terms as county commissioner in the past, but right now he's running for state senate. That's quite a distance from the presidency, of course, and he isn't actually all that ambitious. Politicians have a bad reputation these days, but Miles is simply a man with a sense of duty toward others."

Trudy didn't express her skepticism. He was a minister; he had to believe the best about people.

She looked around at the plain little waiting room with its somewhat shabby furniture. It all came down to this—Jeremy Harper and his family might be comfortable both financially and in their relationships to each other, but right now they were as scared as anybody else. His nephew was seriously hurt, and preacher or not, he was scared. She tried not to be scornful of the kind of religious faith that didn't penetrate into the hard corners of life.

It was better to be like herself, honestly doubting.

"Miles has been good for Betsy," he went on, "though I must admit I wasn't sure at first she wasn't making a mistake. He's a good deal older than she is. But he's given her a good home and been kind to the boys." His voice trailed off.

"Better than lots of marriages." Trudy filled in the gap in the conversation. "Probably better than most."

He turned startled eyes to her. "What?"

She shrugged. "We'd be as well off back in the old days with arranged marriages. Both sides, the man and the woman, want certain things . . . companionship, children, security, whatever. If these were agreed to and planned for in advance—"

"What about love?" It was his turn to interrupt. "You've left that entirely out of the picture, Miss McClung."

A wry twist of her mouth was sufficient to indicate her opinion of romantic love. "My mother was always falling in love," she said, though she didn't often mention her mother. "It was usually of brief duration."

She was almost glad the woman in the green uniform suddenly appeared in the doorway again, stopping the conversation. She didn't know why she'd brought her mother into the conversation; she certainly didn't want to answer questions about her.

"Dr. Harper," the woman said. "Good news this time. Phil is conscious and seems in good condition. He's asking for his mother. We're keeping him in recovery a little longer than usual because of that little problem in surgery. But if you want to bring Mrs. Granbury down, she can see him for a moment." She turned on her heel and walked away, leaving Jeremy standing as though in shock.

"He's going to be all right!" Trudy jumped up and down like a little girl, and he threw his arms around her in a massive hug that reminded her of what he'd said about playing football. They hugged each other joyfully until a loud, throat-clearing noise from close at hand caused them to pull apart abruptly.

The tall, dark-haired beauty who had sung the solo at church that morning stood in the doorway, regarding them with frank disapproval. "Jerry," she said.

Trudy stepped away hastily, hoping she had not hopelessly compromised the minister's reputation. "We've gotten good news about Phil," she said.

"Really?" The word positively dripped icicles. Her dark eyes scrutinized Trudy, then swept dismissingly past her. "I'd heard there was an accident, Jerry. That's why I came over. But I don't know any of the details."

In a few hurried words, Harper explained what

had happened, but words alone were inadequate to convey the horror of the afternoon. Trudy realized that only those who had been at the hospital to experience the dread and the waiting could really know what it had been like. It was almost as though living through the experience together had forged a bond between the man and herself.

Hastily she dismissed the thought. Now that Phil was going to be all right, it wouldn't be necessary for her to spend another minute in his uncle's company.

"I've got to get down to the coffee shop and tell Betsy and Miles," Harper told the black-haired woman. "Phil is asking to see his mother."

"I'll go with you." Melissa tucked a possessive hand around his arm. "Betsy will need friends around her at a time like this."

Trudy stayed right where she was. The other woman's words were deliberately calculated to put her in her place as a stranger. That was exactly where she wanted to be. She had no time to get involved with these people.

"Trudy, aren't you coming?" Harper asked, then looked at the woman at his side. "You two haven't met. Trudy McClung, Melissa Reven."

The two women nodded at each other. "So nice to meet you, Trudy." Melissa was the incarnation of graciousness. "So good of you to look after Jerry in this moment of need. He's always thinking of others, but he doesn't have anyone to look after him."

54

Trudy suspected she knew someone who was ready to fill the vacancy.

Harper made a gesture of impatience. "I've got to tell Betsy. She'll be anxious to see Phil." He looked at Trudy as though waiting for her to join them.

"Go on," she said. "I'll wait here."

He frowned as though to object, but Melissa practically led him away. Trudy watched them go, then picked up her purse and got ready to leave. She'd said she'd wait, but not for how long. By the time they returned, she would be halfway home.

She went out the side door. It had been a most unusual Sunday. But at least she knew now that Phil was out of immediate danger.

Trudy had spent so much of the day in the company of the little boy's family that it was as though a cord bound them and was being stretched as she walked away—a mental cord that kept Trudy thinking about them. She couldn't let that happen. She shook her head to clear it and set her mind on the work that lay ahead in her room. She would have to stay at her desk until late tonight to make up for the time lost today. And she'd hardly made a decent start on the assignment Dr. Lorimer had given her. At the very least, Jeremy Harper owed her a good solid interview after the time she'd invested in his family concerns today.

There she went, thinking about him again! It was natural enough, she supposed, for a woman

55

who'd never had a family of her own to enjoy warming her hands for a few hours in the presence of a close one like his. But that was over now.

She climbed the stairs at home with renewed energy, anxious to get back to work. She frowned to find the door to her room slightly ajar. She'd left it locked. She was sure of that.

A middle-aged woman with graying brown hair and a soft, gentle face sat in the chair behind the desk. She rose as Trudy entered.

"Darling!" she said. "It's so wonderful to see you." She held out her arms and moved toward Trudy.

Trudy circled warily out of reach. This was it. This fading, confused woman was her whole family. "What are you doing here?" She heard the bitter sound in her own voice. "Is it too much, after all you've done, to ask that you leave me alone?"

Tears stood in the woman's doelike brown eyes. She held out a shaking hand. "I've changed, my darling; can't you see that I've changed?"

Chapter Four

Trudy stood, unmoved by either the tears or the emotion in her mother's voice. Instead of answering the appeal, she went to the door and opened it wide.

"You and I have nothing to say to each other." She kept her voice under careful control. "So I'll ask you to leave."

"But Trudy, how can you treat your own mother this way? I know I haven't always been the way I should in the past, but I'm different now. I've sought you out so we can have the kind of relationship a mother and daughter should."

If the door could have been opened wider, Trudy would have done so. Instead she tightened her mouth into a firm line and indicated the door with a tilt of her head. "I have work to do. Good-bye, Dorothy."

"How can you address your own mother as though she were a stranger?" Her mother didn't make a move to leave. "Don't you realize I came here longing to hear myself called Mother by my only baby?"

"I was ten when you told me to call you Dorothy," Trudy said, her voice empty of feeling. "You said it made you feel old to have a half-grown girl as your daughter."

She was beginning to wonder if she was going to have to physically remove her mother from the room, when the chubby, round-faced, and perpetually cheerful woman who was her landlady came singing down the hall.

"Trudy!" She stopped when she saw the young woman in the hall. "I let your mother into your room. I knew you would be so pleased that she'd traveled such a long distance to see you." Even Mrs. Larson's cheerfulness was put under strain by the rigid posture of mother and daughter.

"Dorothy was just leaving," Trudy said, looking at her hesitant parent. The presence of a third party was enough to force her mother to walk reluctantly across the room toward the doorway.

In the hall, she put her hand out to Mrs. Larson. "I'm Dorothy Samuels," she said. "I remarried after Trudy's father died. I'd like to ask you to take good care of my little girl."

Mrs. Larson looked bewildered. "But Trudy has an extra bed in her room. Surely you'll be staying with her while you're in town?"

58

Dorothy turned to look wistfully at her daughter, but the younger woman shook her head. "I'm sure Dorothy has other plans," Trudy said firmly.

Slowly her mother walked down the hall toward the stairs. Trudy listened to the slow thumps as she descended, and finally heard the front door close.

"Trudy!" Mrs. Larson's voice had a note of scolding in it. "We all have our little differences within a family. Goodness knows, my girls and I don't always see eye to eye on things, but a young woman your age should know how much she can hurt her parents."

Trudy stared coldly at the woman. "That person isn't my mother."

Mrs. Larson looked bewildered. "But she said . . ."

Trudy didn't want to talk about it; she didn't even want to think about it. But the look on Mrs. Larson's face disturbed her. None of this was that gentle woman's fault.

"If she comes back, don't let her in my room again," she requested firmly. "She has no right barging into my life."

She went into her room and closed the door. She was proud of herself. She was no longer the little girl who allowed her mother's unexpected appearances to raise a storm of mixed hope and anger inside her.

The appearance of Dorothy Samuels had only been a momentary interruption in her day, nothing more. She sat down at her typewriter and tried to concentrate, methodically beginning to type her impressions of the first pastor she'd met. But her ability to type neatly had deserted her. When she reread that first page, it was so full of mistakes as to be incoherent.

She bent her head down to the desk and wept.

She didn't indulge in the luxury of tears for long, but got up, washed her face, and worked until bedtime, not allowing herself to think about anything else. She went to bed early, but only to relive her childhood dream: She was crossing a narrow bridge across a great chasm, calling for help as she felt herself slipping. But no help came and she was falling, falling . . .

She awakened with a start, unwilling to risk a repetition of the dream that had haunted her at unpredictable intervals for as long as she could remember. She got up, turned on the light and, still wearing pajamas and slippers, went back to her desk and worked until morning.

She didn't even feel sleepy the next day as she went through the routine of her work with students. When Dr. Lorimer stopped her in the hall at midday to ask how the assignment was going, she even had an answer for him.

"I talked to one of the local ministers yesterday," she said. "Dr. Harper."

His deceptively cherubic face beamed suddenly. "Jeremy Harper," he said. "A good place to start. A young man with both brains and feelings, excellent qualities in any profession."

"I didn't know you were a . . . a church person, Dr. Lorimer," Trudy said.

"I'm not. But if I were, Jeremy Harper would be my pastor." He smiled. "I've always had the feeling he was a man you could talk to about your troubles." The smile faded. "But from what I hear, he's having troubles of his own right now."

It took Trudy a moment to grasp what he was talking about. She'd learned a long time ago to shut the things that disturbed her right out of her mind, and almost everything about yesterday was disturbing. "Oh, you mean about the little boy being hurt."

He nodded. "A terrible thing. I'm a crusty old man, well accustomed to the evils of this world. But seeing a child hurt . . . I'll never get used to that."

"I witnessed the accident," Trudy confessed. "It was very upsetting. I'm anxious to learn how Phil is today."

"Get right to work on it then." He looked at his watch. "Aren't you finished with classes for today?" He waited for her response.

Trudy nodded. "I don't have duty at the newspaper this afternoon. I'm free, and could call or go by the church and try to see Dr. Harper. Of course I do have other appointments for interviews."

"I expect that copy to be ready in time for the weekend edition," he warned.

Trudy wasn't at all alarmed. She was accustomed to working under strict deadlines. She thought about calling the church, but decided her second choice was the best one. She would drop by, casually.

The sun was barely visible, only beginning to break through clouds. But Trudy strode briskly along, remembering the walk she'd taken only yesterday with Phil. So much could happen in such a short time.

The massive trees that lined the north edge of the campus were aglow with the changing colors of autumn, and carefully planted chrysanthemums and shasta daisies blossomed in formal flower beds. Trudy walked along, feeling unusually happy for a person who'd only gotten a few hours' sleep the night before. Even the thought that her mother was in town didn't dampen her spirits.

She wondered why she felt so particularly happy. She stopped abruptly in the middle of the sidewalk as a random thought struck her, and was almost hit from behind by a student on a bike.

"Sorry," she apologized hastily even though he was the one at fault, since the bike should have been ridden in the street.

The boy nodded and smiled. After picking up his books, he pedaled on. Trudy proceeded more slowly.

It couldn't be. She couldn't be this happy because she was going to see Jeremy Harper again.

Ridiculous! She tried to push the thought away. The only reason she was going back to the

McFarlin Street Church was because she had to see him for information for her article. She hadn't actually gotten a chance to ask a single question yesterday.

And, of course, she was eager to get an update on Phil's condition. Almost deliberately, she tried to lessen the buoyant bubbles of happiness inside her. There was no reason to feel good today: she had a miserable excuse for an assignment to work on, her mother was in town, poor little Phil was in the hospital recovering from his injuries, and after last night she should be exhausted.

It was the opposite, she supposed, of counting your blessings. But she was determined to keep her feet on the ground. If she was going to feel happy, there had better be a darned good reason why.

She managed to assume the appearance of solemnity by the time she reached the church. She stepped into an empty corridor that seemed to echo oddly. Her heels tapped sharply against the floor as she walked down to the door marked PASTOR'S OFFICE.

She stepped inside. An elderly woman concentrated all her attention on the typewriter in front of her. "There," she finally said, talking to herself. "I managed to get it right." She pulled the sheet of paper from the typewriter and stood up, finally seeing Trudy.

The woman was one of those individuals who smile more with their eyes than with their lips. "Hello," she said. "I didn't hear you come in.

Guess I was making too much noise with my old typewriter. Dr. Jerry keeps saying I need one of those new modern contraptions to type on, but I always tell him I have enough trouble working with this machine I'm used to."

She bustled around efficiently, much like a homemaker welcoming a guest into her house. Before she quite knew what had happened, Trudy found herself seated in a comfortable chair, a cup of delicious coffee in her hand. No questions had been asked yet, not even what her name was.

The little woman, who seemed to be in charge of the office, settled in a chair across from her. "I'm Donita Warren," she said. "Dr. Harper's secretary. Now tell me, dear, what can I do to help you?"

From what she'd seen of Mrs. Warren's typing skills, Trudy had a feeling the friendly little woman hadn't been hired because of her expert secretarial ability. But if it was to give a warm and friendly atmosphere to the pastor's office, then she was succeeding one hundred percent.

"I'm Trudy McClung. I'm doing an article for the student newspaper at the college, which I need to discuss with Dr. Harper."

"You're a student," Mrs. Warren said, speaking as though it were some kind of unusual accomplishment. "All you bright young women these days! What are you studying?"

"I'm in the journalism school," Trudy replied.

"That's the field Dr. Jerry's nephew is majoring in. Steven . . . Steven Granbury.

Perhaps you've met him?"

"I know Steven," Trudy started to explain, "but—"

"Dr. Jerry is over at the hospital now visiting his other nephew. Phil was hurt yesterday, but I'm happy to say he's doing quite well. Dr. Harper should be back in the office any minute now if you'd care to wait."

"I'd be happy to wait for him," Trudy said, pleased to get word of Phil without even having to ask. "You say his nephew is doing well?"

Mrs. Warren was only too pleased to elaborate. She told Trudy all about the accident, the dramatic hours in the hospital, and the good report that had come from the hospital only an hour before when Jeremy had called to tell her he would be in shortly.

"That's so like Dr. Jerry," she went on. "Even in the midst of his own problems, he's conscious of the fact that others might need him."

Trudy was amused. She'd seen devoted employees, but Mrs. Warren deserved some sort of prize. Jeremy Harper had convinced a lot of people of his wonderful qualities.

Trudy's amusement faded. It was sobering to think that for a little while in the cafeteria she'd considered this possible candidate for sainthood as a potential friend. Now she knew she could never be truly relaxed and comfortable in his presence.

The sound of someone approaching from down the hall brought her to her feet. She would talk to him and get her interview over. Then Dr. Lorimer would be happy, and she wouldn't have to see the minister again.

But the figure that appeared in the doorway was that of the dark-haired girl from yesterday. She didn't look past Mrs. Warren.

"I stopped by to get Jerry to take me to lunch," she told the older woman in a no-nonsense voice. "He must be exhausted after spending the night at the hospital, and I hope you realize, Donita, that he wasn't kept there only because of Phil. He was trying to assist a family whose grandmother had died, and they weren't even members here at McFarlin."

Melissa Reven's dark eyes finally landed on Trudy. She brushed past the secretary. "Hello again," she said. "I didn't expect to find you here." She turned back to the secretary. "How does Steven's little friend happen to be here, Donita?"

Trudy felt as though she'd been relegated to the status of a sixteen-year-old as she watched the secretary take a second look at her, then apologize hurriedly. "I am sorry, Miss McClung. There I was babbling on about Dr. Jerry's family, not even realizing you were acquainted."

"I wasn't sure what Miss McClung was doing at the hospital last night," Melissa told Mrs. Warren, "until Betsy explained that she was a friend of Steven's. So good of you to be there to offer your support . . . . Trudy, isn't it?"

Trudy found herself unaccountably furious at a

situation that should have been no more than mildly amusing. She wondered if Jeremy Harper had told his girlfriend that Trudy was his nephew's date. Perhaps it had been the easiest way out of an awkward situation when she'd caught them alone together. Maybe the story hadn't come from Betsy at all.

Dr. Jeremy Harper wasn't quite an unchallenged candidate for sainthood yet.

"If you're here to find out about Phil, I can tell you anything you need to know." Melissa bustled forward, smoothing her immaculate blue tweed skirt into place as she settled herself into the chair Mrs. Warren had recently vacated. "It's not necessary to bother Dr. Jerry, Donita.

"Phil is doing fine," she assured Trudy. "He was scheduled to be moved from intensive care in the middle of the morning. A special nurse will be with him, and the family has been sent home to rest, including Steven, who I'm sure is your principal interest." She laughed lightly.

Trudy smiled. "I'm glad to hear Phil is doing so well," she said, then turned to the secretary, who was watching the two younger women with a vaguely troubled air. "But I will wait to see Dr. Harper on that matter of business we discussed."

Melissa frowned. "Jerry's not here?"

"He phoned that he was spending a little extra time with Phil but would be over soon. I expect him at any minute." The secretary went back to the seat behind her desk, her air of natural friendliness subdued. She seemed aware of the tension in the air.

Trudy recognized it too, but didn't know why it was there. Melissa Reven thought she was Steven's friend, so she shouldn't feel any sense of competition. Trudy wished she could come out and explain that she hadn't the slightest interest in Steven's uncle.

The dark-haired woman leaned forward, her glossy hair swaying gracefully with the motion. "I'm sure your business is terribly important, but my concern is to protect Jerry."

"Protect him?" Trudy allowed her eyebrows to rise questioningly.

"He gives so much of himself. He needs someone to see that he gets a chance to rest."

Mrs. Warren looked as though she was about to protest, but just then a shabby-looking little boy appeared in the doorway. "Can I talk to somebody?" he whispered in a frightened voice.

"Certainly, dear," Mrs. Warren responded in motherly fashion. "Come right in."

Dark eyes glanced from her to the two younger women. "Could it be kind of private?" he asked, still sounding terrified. "I can't talk in front of a crowd."

Trudy tried not to stare, knowing the attention would only alarm the boy more. Donita Warren pulled herself upright and walked out into the hall to place one hand on the child's shoulder. "Come with me. We'll go into the sanctuary and sit down, and you can talk about whatever you like."

68

Trudy frowned, watching them depart. The child looked familiar, yet she didn't know any children.

"Can you imagine anyone letting that boy come into a church looking like that?" Melissa asked. "He was actually dirty."

Trudy hardly heard. She was still trying to place him. But the only boy she knew was Phil, and she'd only met him yesterday. Yesterday! The other boy at the church. Phil's friend.

"Be right back," she said, as though Melissa even cared. She ran out into the hall, looking first one way and then the other, but the woman and boy were nowhere in sight.

Mrs. Warren had said she would take him to the sanctuary. Trudy hardly knew what the word meant but instinctively she walked toward the large auditorium where she'd heard Jeremy Harper speak only yesterday. The woman and the little boy were sitting on a cushioned bench down near the front. They didn't look up as she came in.

Trudy tried to walk as quietly as possible down the carpeted aisle. Church on Sunday morning was very different from church on Monday afternoon. The lights were not turned on, and the colored glass in the long, narrow windows barely admitted any outside light. Golden motes of dust danced in stray sunbeams up near the distant ceiling. It was awesomely quiet, and Trudy felt almost as though she'd strayed into a forbidden place.

Mrs. Warren looked up questioningly as she approached, but Trudy went to the boy.

"You're, Mike," she said. "Phil's friend."

He nodded wordlessly.

"I'm glad you know who he is, Miss Mc-Clung." The secretary brushed impatiently at her skirt. "He said he wanted to talk, but I haven't been able to get him started. Usually I get on well with children; I have three grandchildren of my own. But this boy seems scared of me."

The secretary's intentions were good, Trudy knew, but she couldn't approve of the way she talked about the boy as though he couldn't understand. "Perhaps he'll talk to me," she said, settling down at his side. "Can I help, Mike?"

He nodded again, but still didn't say anything.

"Well then, I'll get back to the office." Mrs. Warren rose to her feet. "Let me know if there's anything I can do."

Trudy watched the sprightly little woman hurry up the long aisle toward the rear of the room before turning to the boy. He was looking down at his hands, both of which were knotted into sturdy little fists. Melissa Reven was right. His clothing was torn and dirty. And Trudy had a feeling he knew how to use those fists. But the look in his eyes was another thing.

"Don't be afraid." She touched his shoulder and he pulled away. "Don't you remember me?"

He gave her a searching look. "Sure. You're the lady who sat next to us in church yesterday, the one Phil told to sit down."

He was silent again, and Trudy looked across at the polished wood of the organ rather than at him, giving him time to collect his thoughts so he could say what he wanted.

"Phil's uncle should be here soon if you'd rather talk to him," she suggested, aware of her inexperience in dealing with children. She had offered to help when she saw the fear in this child's eyes. But now that she thought about it . . .

He shook his head. "He's the one who's the preacher. I'd be ascared of what he'd say."

"You don't have to be afraid of me." Trudy tried to smile. She knew too well what it was like to be a forlorn, outcast child with no one to talk to. "Did you come here because you were worried about Phil?"

He nodded. This time his eyes didn't avoid her face, but watched her closely.

"He's going to be all right. He's in the hospital now and getting the best of care."

"Are you lying?"

Trudy grinned. This was something the gently reared church secretary or even its pastor might not understand. But she remembered well enough that instinctive, and often justified, distrust of adults.

"I have it on the best authority."

He gave her the once-over again, his eyes narrowed in distrust. "You must be lying," he said, "because the car hit him hard, and then he laid awful still. I think he's dead."

The last few years of her life had been spent working with words. Yet at this moment, Trudy didn't know what to say. How to convince the boy of the truth?

She heard some slight sound from the back of the room and hoped Mrs. Warren wasn't choosing exactly the wrong moment to come back. But she didn't turn around. She was afraid to take her eyes from Mike. His thin legs trembled as though ready for flight.

"Phil was seriously hurt, Mike. I wouldn't try to deceive you about that. He was taken to the hospital in an ambulance, and he had to have emergency surgery. But he's much better today. He's going to be all right." She spoke in slow tones to give weight to each word.

But he wasn't a child to believe anything easily. Creases puckered his forehead. "Did you see him yourself?"

"Not today," Trudy admitted. "But I was told—"

"You can't believe everything people say," he interrupted.

"That's true," Trudy agreed, "but in this case—"

Again he interrupted. "It's real important. Phil's my friend, and I try to look after him because he's not as old as me." His voice sank to a whisper so low she barely made out the last words. "It's my fault the car hit him."

Trudy nearly jumped out of her skin when she felt a hand rest briefly against her back. She looked up to find Jeremy Harper standing above her.

"Phil was injured by accident," he told the boy. "Nobody was at fault."

The boy stared, his eyes enormous. Trudy reached out to grab one of his hands, certain he was about to take off running.

"Mike, this is Phil's uncle."

"I know. He's the preacher man." Mike tugged at his hand, trying to free himself.

"You can't leave yet," Trudy told him. "We've got to talk first."

He looked from her to the tall man, then pointed one finger of his free hand up at Jeremy. "I'll talk to you, but not to him."

"Come here, Mike." She tried to pull him closer, but he wouldn't allow it. "We want to help you."

He pulled away, allowing her only to hold his hand. "I don't need that gushy stuff. I'm too old."

He didn't look very old to Trudy, but if he thought he was too grown up to be offered comfort, then he was. Even a child had a right to dignity.

"How old are you, Mike?" Jeremy asked.

"Eight. I'll be nine next May."

"Eight," the pastor repeated. "You're only a year older than Phil. You shouldn't feel responsible for him. Why, Mike, there was no way you could have prevented that accident. Trudy and I were driving up as it happened, and there wasn't a

73

thing *we* could do to stop it."

The little boy stared in distrust. Jeremy sat down on the bench at Trudy's side as though to make the child more comfortable by approaching him more nearly at his own physical level.

Mike looked again at Trudy. "I won't talk to him."

"He would know better what to tell you," Trudy protested, anxious to have someone more experienced in dealing with pain work with the boy. "I'm sure Dr. Harper can help you."

"I'd better go." The boy tried to pull his hand free, but Trudy hung on stubbornly. Mike needed help, and she was going to see he got it whether he wanted it or not.

"Perhaps if I stepped back out into the hall," Harper suggested, "he'd feel free to talk."

"You don't have to do that," Mike told him, scowling. "I can whisper in her ear. Then she can tell you, and you can tell the police if you like."

"That sounds fair," Harper told him, man to man.

"Police?" Trudy echoed in dismay. What did the boy think he'd done?

Mike bent closer to put his mouth to her ear, looking suspiciously at the minister before beginning to whisper. Harper drew away about a foot farther, glancing in the other direction as though he wasn't even interested.

"It was my fault the kid got hurt," Mike whispered.

Trudy frowned. "Why do you think that?"

He whispered again. "Because of Blackie."

"Blackie?" she asked out loud.

"Shhhhhh." He frowned, tilting his head toward Harper. "He'll hear you."

She nodded and waited for the next whisper.

"Blackie's my pup. Phil was playing with him, and he ran into the street."

Finally Trudy understood. The little black puppy that ran in front of the red car was Blackie.

She reached out and hugged the wiggling, protesting little boy. "It wasn't your fault, Mike."

He pulled away. He looked at Harper. "You can tell him now. I'm ready for him to call the police."

Chapter Five

Trudy would have laughed if the boy hadn't been so heartbreakingly serious. He truly believed he'd committed a crime.

She looked at Jeremy. "He thinks he was responsible for Phil getting hurt because the dog that Phil chased after belongs to him."

"Name's Blackie." Manfully he faced the minister. "My mom don't know I've got him. I keep him in the old shed out back."

Trudy touched Jeremy's arm in warning, afraid he would show amusement. But he didn't, not by so much as a flicker of an eyelash.

"Your pup," he told Mike thoughtfully, seeming to review the facts. "How long have you had him?"

"A week. Somebody dumped him. People do that with puppies sometimes. He was starving."

"Been taking good care of him?"

"Sure." The boy nodded. "He's my puppy. I feed him scraps, and I'm doing jobs so I can get him the shots he needs."

Jeremy looked at Trudy. "What do you think?"

"Sounds responsible to me," she replied.

The boy pulled his hand free and stepped back. "But it was because of Blackie that Phil got hurt. I keep him in the shed when I can't look after him. But Phil came over and wanted to play. I was watching, but I looked away for a minute; then I heard Phil yell, and when I turned around he was running into the street after Blackie." He swallowed with visible effort. "I saw people running up, and I knew they'd take care of Phil . . . and so I ran away 'cause I was scared and I knew Blackie was too, and I had to find him."

Trudy wished she could offer some comfort, but Harper looked stern. "Stick around and face things next time," he said. "It's usually less painful." He turned to Trudy. "The way I see it, nobody could be responsible for a puppy getting away like that. They move fast. It could have happened to anybody."

She nodded. "I agree."

He looked at the boy. "It wasn't your fault that Phil got hurt, Mike. But you do need to start training your puppy to come when called. It'd probably be a good idea to get one of those long chains so you can get him out of that shed and into the fresh air even when you can't be right with him."

Mike stared. "You're saying it's really not my fault?" He shook his head. "And you must really know, since you're Phil's uncle and a preacher and all that."

Jeremy Harper grinned. "You can stop worrying about it. And as soon as Phil is better, I'll take you over to visit him."

The boy nodded. "I'll try to get some extra jobs so I can buy that chain for Blackie like you said."

"No need." Harper shrugged. "I'm sure we've got the very thing you need lying around here someplace." He gestured around the church as though such items were in common use. "We have a really long chain that will allow the pup to roam all over the yard and still be safely confined."

The boy eyed him suspiciously. "If you're sure you won't need it."

"You'll be doing us a favor by putting it to good use," Harper assured him. "I'll locate it and bring it over to you tomorrow if that's okay."

"Sure," the boy agreed, his expression gradually brightening. He looked as though he was having trouble taking everything in. He started to walk out, then turned around. "Be sure and tell Phil I said hi."

"We'll do that," Harper agreed. "Stop by the office and give your address to my secretary so I know where to drop off that chain."

The boy nodded, then disappeared into the darkness of the hall.

Trudy touched Jeremy's hand. "You handled that exactly right. You treated the matter seriously. A lot of people would have brushed his worries aside, and he might have gone on feeling guilty about Phil's accident for years."

He grinned. "You were doing okay yourself, Miss McClung. Did anybody ever tell you how nice you are?"

She jerked her hand away. "I got trapped into the situation. I happened to come into a church on a Sunday morning, just as part of my job, and was seated next to a couple of small boys. And look what it's gotten me into!"

"Not everyone likes to hear me speak, but I've never heard it referred to as an actual job before."

Hastily she explained the nature of her assignment, and Dr. Lorimer's insistence that she do an interview with him.

He nodded. "Have you had lunch?"

For an instant, Trudy couldn't recall. "No," she finally admitted. "I was too busy."

He got up and extended his hands to pull her to her feet. "I seem to remember promising you a picnic. Unfortunately I've got a couple of calls to make later this afternoon, so we can't go to the state park."

"That's all right," Trudy assured him, indignant because he spoke as though she were a child promised ice cream as a treat. "I haven't

79

been staying awake nights counting on a picnic at the state park. As a matter of fact, I have things to do.''

"But interviewing me is part of your job,'' he informed her, a wicked twinkle in his eyes. "And Gerald Lorimer is an old friend of mine.''

"Impossible,'' she insisted firmly. "Dr. Lorimer doesn't have friends. He was hatched whole and vicious.''

Jeremy laughed. "In spite of the impression he likes to give up at the college, he's not a bad guy. Still, I wouldn't want you to encounter his wrath if you failed to turn in assigned work. So I'll sacrifice my time.'' He moved down the aisle in long strides, and Trudy had little choice but to run to keep up. "We'll stop by my office and make sure young Mike left his address. I wouldn't want to lose touch with him. Don't know what his circumstances at home are, but obviously he could use a couple of friends.''

"And a chain so his dog can come out of that shed once in a while.'' Trudy told herself that if she was going to go around in the company of Dr. Jeremy Harper, she would have to take up jogging again just to keep up with him.

She waited outside the office, taking advantage of the pause to catch her breath.

"Donita,'' she heard him say as he went in. "Oh, Melissa, where's Donita?''

Then Trudy followed him into the office. Melissa Reven was sitting at the secretary's desk, leafing through a stack of typed papers. "You're

80

still here, Miss McClung?" She smiled sweetly.

Trudy smiled back. "Still here," she confirmed.

Melissa turned her attention to the minister. "Donita had to do a couple of errands," she said. "I assured her I'd be perfectly capable of answering the phones for her while she was out."

"Did a little boy stop by here and leave his address?" Harper asked, not looking particularly pleased at the temporary change in staff.

"If you mean that same urchin who was here before, he peeked his head in, but he took off like a frightened mouse when I inquired what his business was. You've simply got to be more careful, Jerry. You know how many churches are being burglarized these days."

Annoyance flickered across his face, but he didn't correct her. "I'm going out with Miss McClung for a while, Melissa. If anyone calls, you can say I'll be back around five."

"But where can I reach you?" she asked, poising a pen over a piece of paper.

"You can't," he told her. "I'll be out of contact."

She didn't like that, Trudy could tell. But Melissa didn't object. "I'm not sure how Steven will like you taking his girl out." She spoke in a kittenish tone.

"Steven?" Jeremy asked with a frown.

"Betsy told me how taken he was with Miss McClung." The tall brunette smiled at the smaller girl. "And I have to admit she's terribly cute."

Trudy felt as if she should be wearing a cheer-leader's skirt and yelling, "Go, team! Go!" She wondered if Melissa would accept a birth certificate as evidence of her age.

"Dr. Harper and I are going out on a business matter," she said. "Nothing Steven would object to."

She thought Jeremy glanced at her oddly. Maybe he didn't like the idea of his young nephew being interested in an older woman. It was funny, considering that she and Steven barely knew each other outside the classroom. In fact, she hadn't even recognized him until after Phil's accident.

"I have to make a call before we leave," he said. "I'll only be a minute."

He vanished into an inner office, and Trudy settled herself on the arm of a chair. Melissa looked at her, and Trudy had an uncomfortable feeling that the other woman didn't approve of people who sat on the arms of chairs.

She moved over and sat down properly, putting her feet together neatly and not even crossing her legs. She was prim as a statue.

"Jerry's so sweet," Melissa told her.

Trudy thought about that. "I don't know if 'sweet' is the word I would have used."

"But then you hardly know him." Melissa got up from behind the desk, coming around to speak in more confidential tones. "I don't want you to get the wrong impression. Women do, sometimes. It's quite a problem for a bachelor minister."

Trudy grinned. "Even more of a problem for a married one."

Melissa looked shocked. "I'm sure no one could seriously misunderstand Jerry's—Dr. Harper's intentions. But I wanted you to understand exactly what the situation is, particularly with poor Steven involved. Young men that age are so vulnerable."

It was quite funny; nobody had ever considered Trudy a dangerous woman before, and now she was suspected of trying to make off with two men at once.

"Steven is obviously popular with the girls around campus," she assured Melissa. "You don't need to worry about his affections."

"His mother assured me he has quite a crush on you. He talks about you all the time, she said."

"It's not unusual in the student-teacher relationship," Trudy observed dryly. "They soon get over it."

"Teacher?" Melissa Reven's face did not wear a frown well. The placid features were meant only for smiling.

"I'm a graduate assistant and Steven is one of my students," Trudy told her.

"A graduate assistant?" Melissa laughed. "For a moment I thought you meant you were a real teacher."

Trudy smiled even though it was hard. "Maybe I'd better wait for Dr. Harper out in the hall." She had a feeling he wouldn't approve if he came out and found she'd tossed a book at his girl-friend. No point standing around letting Melissa tempt her to rashness.

"Just a minute." Melissa's expression was suddenly serious. "There's something else I want you to know."

Trudy had little choice but to wait. She could hear the sound of Jeremy's voice from the inner office.

"I understand about you and Steven and wish the best for you. I know what it's like to be in love." She lifted her lovely shoulders in an elegant shrug. "Jerry and I have been so happy."

Trudy's eyes narrowed thoughtfully. It was as if Melissa hadn't absorbed a word she'd said about Steven. The truth was that she was being warned off the uncle, not the nephew. Trudy felt like a kid who has a hard time resisting a dare.

"How nice," she said, "that you and Dr. Harper *have been* so close." The emphasis she used made it obvious she considered Melissa's relationship with the minister to be a thing of the past.

Melissa was a little slow. It took an instant for her to catch on. Then her dark eyes sparked fire. "Jeremy Harper and I are engaged, Miss Mc-Clung."

Trudy knew these were rashly spoken words. If she'd been a gambling woman, she'd have put money against the existence of a formal engagement. "How nice," she said again. "I must

84

congratulate Jeremy as soon as he finishes his call."

The dark eyes met hers. Melissa Reven knew a challenge when she heard one and was not easily intimidated. "It isn't exactly a formal engagement," she admitted. "We haven't told anyone yet."

"You told me," Trudy reminded her sweetly. She didn't know why she was taking this attitude. It was no business of hers if Jeremy Harper chose this polished beauty as his wife, except for the instinctive feeling she had that Melissa didn't really even know Jeremy Harper, much less love him.

She remembered the way he'd looked at the hospital last night after draining himself of strength in order to offer a full measure of comfort to others. He needed more than Melissa Reven as a wife.

Melissa finally controlled her anger. "The only reason I confided in you, Miss McClung—"

Trudy interrupted. "Oh, call me Trudy. It's easier to say."

"I only told you about Jerry and me because I don't want you to be hurt."

"You were trying to protect me? Your fiancé has a reputation for giving too much attention to the ladies, and you wanted me to know his intentions could never be serious because it was you he truly loved?"

Trudy's attempt at humor was entirely lost on Melissa. A look of utter horror came into the perfect face. But before she could deny the accusation, Trudy realized that Jeremy had returned and was standing in the doorway of his office, listening to every word being said. Melissa's back was turned to him; she didn't even know he was there.

"Jerry is a wonderful person," Melissa protested hurriedly. "A fine man and a fine minister. I look up to him. I worship him. How can you suggest such things about a man?"

One long home run for Melissa. What would any man prefer? To be teased and laughed at, or to be worshiped? And it had been spoken so honestly. Melissa didn't even know he was standing there.

Trudy felt ashamed she'd entered into the mock competition with the other woman. Melissa really cared. Trudy was only playing games. She smiled at Melissa. "Here's Dr. Harper now," she said. "So we can get on with our interview. Don't worry, Melissa. I won't keep him away from you long."

She walked with him out to his car. Neither of them said a word until the little car was gliding down the street away from the church.

"Nice of you to hand me over to Melissa that way," he said. "You might at least have put up a fight."

"Egotist." She grinned up at him. "Besides, I have other interests." He couldn't know she meant her career.

"Steven?" he questioned. "His mom's been

telling me that he's talked of nothing but you since school started this semester."

There was no point in denying it. They all persisted in believing she had romantic interests in Steven, so there was no reason to embarrass the boy by pointing out that it was a one-sided situation that would soon wear off.

She shrugged, not answering. "You don't appreciate Melissa," she accused. "She's the most beautiful woman I've ever seen, and she's crazy about you."

"You sound like Betsy," he retorted lightly. "Why are women always trying to marry men off?"

She didn't know the answer to that since she had no intention of marrying herself. "Ministers usually marry. Wives help in their work. They play the piano, lead the women's groups, teach Sunday school class."

He grinned down at her. "Volunteering for the position?"

She almost used a familiar expletive from her childhood, one he could not possibly have approved of. "Hardly. I have no musical ability, and if I tried to teach Sunday school . . . well, I know about Noah and the flood and the parting of the Red Sea, but that's just about the total extent of my biblical knowledge. I acquired that during the three months I was placed with an elderly woman who attended the Methodist church each Sunday. The rest of the time I didn't have church families."

87

"Families?" he asked, looking puzzled. "In the plural?"

She forgot that she hadn't meant to bring that up. It always made her sound like Little Orphan Annie asking for sympathy. "After my father died, I was brought up in a series of foster homes." She smiled. "Perfect upbringing for a future journalist—lots of variety!"

He didn't smile. "What about your mother?"

Trudy didn't want to talk about her. To mention that she was in town could only bring up a host of other questions. She dodged the question hastily. "She died too. Anyway, I'm supposed to be the interviewer here, and you're asking all the questions."

"Sorry," he apologized. "But we can get to work seriously once we get to Seven Oaks."

They had reached the edge of town and were driving into open country. "Seven Oaks?" Trudy asked with a frown.

"It's the old Granbury home. People don't go in much for naming things in this country, but the Granburys always liked to do things differently. It was named, the story goes, by the first Mrs. Granbury, a pioneer lady who hailed from the South."

"And it has oaks around the house?" Trudy asked.

"Not anymore. There's lots of trees, oaks even, though I don't know where the number seven comes from. Maybe she just thought it sounded like a good name."

Trudy glanced at her watch. "But I don't have

much time, and I wanted to take you out for lunch."

"I called Mildred, the cook at Seven Oaks, and asked her to put up a picnic hamper for us. We'll eat down by the creek, and you can interview me in beautiful solitude."

Trudy wasn't about to admit that the thought of Jeremy Harper and all that solitude was a little threatening. "Sounds lovely," she said, "but you must remember I haven't much time. I have a couple more interviews this evening."

"We'll get back in plenty of time. In fact, I might be able to help you line up the rest of the information you need. People in the churches in a town this size usually know each other fairly well. I'd be glad to introduce you around."

They turned into a long tree-lined driveway. It wasn't until they made the last turn that Trudy finally saw the house and the grounds that surrounded it. It was a white mansion with columns in the Southern-plantation style, impeccably maintained with well-groomed lawns stretching into wooded countryside.

"Seven Oaks," she said, feeling a little awed. Somehow she'd never expected anything like this. "Your sister married this?"

He shook his head. "She married Miles Granbury," he corrected patiently. "He's an exceptional man and doesn't need these trappings to be a fine husband."

"But he's so much older than your sister," Trudy pointed out, her eyes still on the scene ahead. As an interviewer, she knew well enough how to ask the loaded question, but this one was spoken innocently, popping out of her mind before she could stop it. She reached across to touch his arm. "I'm sorry," she said. "It's none of my business."

"Age difference is an relevant subject," he answered lightly. "Look at you and Steven."

"Yes," she agreed. "Look at me and Steven. Here I am practically an elderly woman, and he's a mere college sophomore." She got out of the car and went with him into the house. It was no echoing fortress from the past, but had been carefully modernized so as to preserve the flavor of its history and add the comforts of the present.

Mildred Foxmore, the cook, handed an enormous hamper to Jeremy, but her curious glance rested on Trudy.

Jeremy introduced them. "Miss McClung is interviewing me," he said. "She works for the newspaper at the college."

"It's a lovely day . . . for interviewing." Mrs. Foxmore smiled benignly at them, her skeptical gaze indicating she wasn't buying the story at all.

Jeremy stowed the hamper in the car, and they drove on past the house, parking to the side of a little private road that led into the wooded pastureland in the back. He carried the hamper down toward a little creek that wound through the pasture.

Mildred was right. It was lovely out. The earlier gloom and clouds had melted under the gentle autumn sun, and it had become a remarkable day.

Trudy put her briefcase down on the grassy bank of the creek and indulged in a sigh. "We should have done the interview right in your office," she said. "This seems almost sinful."

His eyebrows rose challengingly. "What did you have in mind?" he asked.

He was laughing at her. Trudy blushed as she hurried to explain. "I only meant that with poor little Phil in the hospital and other people working at their jobs, it seems unprofessional to be conducting an interview in a beautiful spot like this. I'm not sure Dr. Lorimer would approve."

He opened the hamper and took out a cloth, spreading it on the grass. "I've known Gerald Lorimer since I moved to this part of the state, and I don't think he would object to anything that gets the story he wants. He has a single-track mind."

Trudy sat down carefully on the grass. "The same thing might be said of me. My career is the only thing that really matters to me."

He didn't comment, but began putting food out on the cloth. Trudy watched as thick steak sandwiches, a thermos of hot chocolate, bunches of grapes, and slices of homemade pound cake were spread before them.

"It's hard to concentrate on work under these circumstances," she protested.

He smiled at her. His striking coloring—the tawny gold hair, bronzed skin, and deep blue eyes

—sparkled with technicolor vividness in the afternoon sun.

Hurriedly Trudy opened her briefcase. She had to get her mind on business. "I like to use a tape recorder," she told him, inserting fresh batteries as she talked. "But some subjects clam up totally at the idea. Would you prefer that I just take notes?"

"The recorder won't bother me." He took a bite of his sandwich and poured chocolate into two cups, handing one to her. "Fire away."

Trudy had never felt so at a loss as to how to begin an interview. She couldn't seem to come up with a single question. She fumbled through her case, conscious of his watching eyes on her, until she found the notebook that contained the list of questions she'd prepared.

She took a sip of chocolate. "How long have you been in the ministry, Dr. Harper?" she asked.

His grin was disarming. "Thought we'd finally moved up to Jeremy."

She tried to relax. "Jeremy," she corrected.

He leaned back against the trunk of a tree. "This is a unique opportunity. It's not often a man gets to talk about himself without being accused of boring his listener to death."

"I won't be bored," Trudy assured him.

"And if you are"—he closed his eyes—"you won't admit it."

"The question, Jeremy. Answer the question." At this rate her time would be all gone, and she wouldn't have a bit of information about him.

"I've only been a minister for six years. I'd finished college and spent a year or so doing other things before I gave in to the call."

"Gave in?" Trudy was puzzled. The tape recorder whirred softly in the background.

"I'd known since I was a boy that God had called me for special service. But I had plans of my own."

Trudy didn't understand what he meant. "What kind of plans?"

He shrugged. "I wanted to play football, and I was fairly good at it. I got a scholarship to college and thought I was headed straight into a professional career."

"Something happened to interfere with your plans," Trudy guessed. "You got hurt or you weren't as good as you thought. Lots of us find the path we would have chosen wasn't practical. There was a time when my goal in life was to be a movie star."

"True enough," he agreed, not sounding as though giving up his hopes for a football career had been particularly crushing.

"So you compromised," Trudy urged, trying to get him to go on talking. "When you found out you couldn't do anything much in professional football, you did this instead."

The lazy look vanished from his face. "Compromised!" He sounded distinctly annoyed at the word. His forehead creased into multiple frown lines, and the blue eyes flashed.

Trudy put her sandwich down and leaned closer

to him. "Go ahead and admit it," she said. "People have a right to know their ministers are human like everyone else. They'll be interested to learn you've had to give up your dreams too."

His hand reached out and gripped hers so hard that it hurt, and his face was a thundercloud of anger. "Don't tell me what I thought or what I think." His voice wasn't loud, but it was intense with concentrated rage. "I've never had much use for people telling me what my motivations were."

He released her hand, jumped up and stalked down to the creek, staring down into the trickling stream of water. Trudy watched in dismay. What had she said to set off fireworks?

It was hardly more than sixty seconds before he returned to her side. His smile was apologetic. "Sorry," he said. "But going into the ministry wasn't second choice." He grinned again, but with genuine humor this time. "In fact, it wasn't my choice at all, not for a long time. But when I did decide, it was all the way."

This was the strangest interview Trudy had ever conducted. She didn't seem to be in charge at all; it was simply flowing along, taking unnatural twists and turns like a flooded river. The answers he gave raised more questions than they answered.

"Didn't mean to lose my temper," he told her, looking like a small boy caught in petty domestic crime like cookie snatching. "Never do. But still, in spite of my best efforts, it slips out sometimes."

"I didn't even realize you had a temper," she

confessed. "It's the first display I've witnessed."

He shrugged. "When I was a kid, it was quite a problem for me—an inherited trait apparently. My mother was noted for her rages, but she was a small woman and I was a particularly large boy, and my anger had a tendency to do considerably more damage than hers. I'd seen her learn to control her temper and was determined to do the same. But it's a continuing struggle."

His tone was light, but somehow Trudy was able to understand that he spoke from deep-rooted sincerity.

"I get mad slowly," Trudy admitted. "But when it happens, look out. People have been known to flee from all adjacent counties."

He smiled. "I'll try to remember not to make you mad," he said. He reached to take her hand once again, but instead of the firm grip of moments before, his touch was gentle. If he had been any other man, she would have suspected that he was about to make a pass.

He released her hand, but only to get up and come around to sit on her side of the tablecloth. "You're a most fetching young lady, Miss Mc-Clung," he told her, taking her hand into his again. He bent and would have kissed her except that she moved away so quickly.

There was no question about it. Jeremy Harper was definitely not a candidate for sainthood.

Chapter Six

Trudy didn't know why she was so disappointed to find that the young pastor of the McFarlin Street Church was an ordinary human being. She was used to disillusionment.

"I suppose I owe you another apology," he told her. "But I've waited years for you, and now that you're here . . ." He didn't finish the sentence, but grinned down at her, reminding her once more of his younger nephew.

"You waited for me?" Trudy asked, not even beginning to understand. "That doesn't make sense."

He reached for her hand, but she doubled both hands into fists.

"I'm a romantic at heart," he spoke lightly. "I believe there's a woman designed by God for each man and vice versa. I always knew I'd recognize right away when I'd found her."

Trudy stared at him. He wasn't simply human. He was also out of his mind. "What about Melissa?" she asked.

"Melissa?" He sounded genuinely puzzled.

"She's in love with you."

He shook his head. "Melissa is in love with what she sees as me, the pastor of her church, the man who stands up front each Sunday and tries to interpret the words of God. It's something like the kid who gets a crush on a favorite teacher."

"It's easy enough for you to dismiss her feelings," she accused, suddenly feeling like crying. She knew how Melissa felt. It would be nice to believe there were still strong, honorable men, men who were concerned with things greater than their own gratifications.

"What would you have me do?" he asked reasonably. "I can't marry her simply because it's what she wants. It has to be a two-sided thing. Besides, I love you."

It was as though he'd said the sun was shining or the water in the creek was still running. His love was like that, an immutable law of nature.

Unconsciously Trudy reached over to click off the tape recorder, turning to find herself being taken into his arms. She didn't protest, didn't even seem to want to protest, as his lips touched hers, at first gently, then with surging masculine strength. Trudy had always denied herself this kind of release, not because of some dream of a great love, but because she knew love to be a trap that would earn her only the kind of life that had been her mother's. But now she was past logic and responded freely to the warmth of his lips. He was the one who finally pulled away.

His face was only inches from hers, and he looked down at her as though he couldn't see enough of her face. It was almost embarrassing, and Trudy tried to edge away, but he put his hands on her shoulders.

"I love you," he said.

"You already told me that," she protested shakily.

"I plan to tell you frequently," he assured her, "for the rest of our lives."

Trudy felt as though her insides had turned to jelly. She tried to draw her wits together. "I've got two interviews this evening," she said, falling back on work as usual. "And I haven't any idea what time it is."

He reached down to her hand, peering at the watch on her wrist. "It's ten after five."

"I have an interview at five-thirty." She shook herself free and stood up, welcoming the excuse. She didn't like this feeling of not being completely in charge of her emotions. She wouldn't allow her feelings to make decisions that should be made by her intellect.

"If it's that important." He hesitated, giving her ample opportunity to say that the appointment could be postponed. But now that she was on her feet, Trudy was anxious to get away. She began to gather their picnic things together.

"Tell Mildred everything was delicious," she said, not looking at him.

"You hardly ate a thing."

"Too much was happening, and I didn't even get my interview. I'll have to talk to you again."

"You needn't sound as though that's the world's worst chore."

She didn't answer, but put notebook and tape recorder back into the case. "You wouldn't think it funny if you had an assignment that had to be handed in before the end of the week and you hadn't managed to get a single bit of usable information." Her voice sounded dangerously close to tears, and Trudy told herself there was no excuse for getting so emotional over an incomplete interview. She refused even to allow her brain to think about the other things that had happened this afternoon to stir her feelings.

"We can talk in the car on the way back," he told her, suddenly formal. "I'll be glad to give you the information you need."

She nodded, starting up the creek bank, her briefcase in one hand. He stopped her with a touch on the shoulder.

"I didn't plan it this way. I'd hoped that if we could gradually get acquainted, you might come to have at least a casual liking for my dull self." He grinned, but she couldn't manage to smile. "Have I ruined everything by rushing you so, darling?"

It was his use of the endearment that reminded Trudy of her mother. She had always called her

99

darling on the rare visits she'd made. She was always warm and affectionate, always either in love, or falling out of or into a new love. Her life was ruled by her emotions. Trudy had resolved a long time ago that she would never be like that.

She looked coldly at Jeremy Harper. "You're an attractive man," she told him. "I can't help being drawn to you . . . on a physical level."

He smiled gently, his eyes warm. "That's a good place to start. I'm willing to devote hours and hours to convincing you the attraction goes deeper."

She shook her head. She pulled away and started once again toward the car. No use talking to him. He'd never understand.

"We're wrong for each other," she shouted back down the hill at him. "Entirely wrong."

"Who says?" He snatched up the picnic hamper and started up toward her. She was reminded of what he'd said about his quick temper.

She walked faster, seeing that he was quickly gaining ground in spite of the heavy hamper that swung from his arm. She broke into a run. She raced for the car and reached the door as he caught up with her, placing one large hand against the door so she couldn't open it.

"Who says we're wrong for each other?" he demanded, his voice angry.

"I do." She faced him bravely, feeling particularly small in spite of her usual high heels. "You have one kind of life, and I have another.

You're the pastor of a church, with enormous responsibilities to other people." Her voice had suddenly turned earnest as she tried to explain. "I have only myself, but my life is important to me. I could never be what you need in a wife."

His anger was suddenly gone. "How can you know what I need?"

"Someone like Melissa—someone who sings in church and knows how to talk religion and isn't likely to come out with an embarrassing word that stuck in her head somewhere in the unfortunate years of her childhood." She pushed past him to open the door, then climbed inside. "I'll never get back in time for my interview unless you hurry."

His anger was back, and she watched, impressed with the way he managed to subdue it. While he drove the car, she peppered him with the appropriate questions. By the time they'd gotten back to town, she knew all the things she needed to know, the vital statistics of Jeremy Harper's life. With these, she'd be able to write her story.

He let her out at the little Baptist church where she was already over fifteen minutes late for her appointment, and she went inside to find the elderly minister waiting patiently for her.

"No need to apologize." He waved aside her explanations. "Got here only a couple of minutes ago myself. Had an unexpected call from one of our members who was hospitalized."

Hospitals, illness, death. It seemed to Trudy that ministers dealt with nothing but sadness. She wondered how Jeremy could stand it.

Chapter Seven

The newsroom of the *Daily* was a beehive of activity that Trudy watched with the eyes of a hawk, trying to make sure that each student was handling his or her part of the assigned work. Deadlines were fast approaching for the weekend edition.

She stopped at one desk to help a neophyte who was panicking at the thought of the approaching deadline. "Just write it," she said. "The story has to be ready on time."

The pretty blonde with enormous violet eyes stared helplessly up at her. "But, Miss McClung, I'm not sure it'll be any good. I don't know how to begin."

Trudy grinned. "At this point," she said, waving one hand in the direction of the clock on the back wall, "you don't worry about good. You

102

worry about on time."

"But, Miss McClung!"

"A good reporter never misses a deadline, Ashli." Trudy allowed sternness to creep into her voice. She remembered all too well the feeling this girl was experiencing. It still hit her sometimes—a frozen, miserable fright that could keep her from producing a word if she let it take control of her mind. "Start writing your story," she said. "And do the best you can."

She strolled on, stopping to break up horseplay between two sophomores, directing them back to the task at hand. Steven Granbury was at the next desk, his head bent down in strict concentration. He was turning out to be a better student than she'd anticipated. She moved by without speaking.

"Miss McClung?"

She turned back. He smiled shyly. "We haven't seen much of you this week. Phil keeps asking for you."

"I'll try to stop by," Trudy promised vaguely. She was fonder already of Phil than was good for her and had no intention of allowing herself to be drawn further into the web of the Granbury-Harper charm.

Jeremy Harper had called the house several times. So had her mother. They were the only people she didn't want to talk to, so she'd been careful to spend as much time as possible at school. Trudy went back to her desk, but had barely looked down at her own work when she became conscious of a commanding presence at her elbow.

Dr. Gerald Lorimer didn't have to cough or clear his throat to announce his entrance. Somehow his strong personality automatically made her aware of him. Trudy looked at him expectantly.

He waved a stack of papers in her face. "Not bad," he said.

Trudy blinked. "My research article?"

He nodded and she managed a smile. She knew enough from listening to the campus grapevine to realize that anything vaguely resembling a compliment was to be cherished when spoken by the resident ogre. In fact, anything short of outright insults was so much to the good.

"Your writing is coherent," he informed her grudgingly, "and the research is thorough, especially considering the length of time in which you had to work."

"Thanks." Trudy stammered out the word, still afraid the insults were waiting in the wings. "I dreaded the assignment, but I did get involved once I started work."

He nodded his understanding. "I like the way you got them to tell it the way it was with a minimum of whitewash—their difficulties and discouragements as well as the inspirational moments. You represented them as real people. Not superhumans, but people who look through mistakes and difficulties to . . ." He hesitated, frowning down at the paper. "It's most convincing."

"I wasn't trying to persuade anyone to a particular viewpoint." Trudy held up a hand in protest. "In fact if you got the whole group of individuals I interviewed into a room together, there'd probably be one colossal argument because they seem to see a lot of different routes to God. And yet they seemed, most of them, to share some special vision. . . ."

She stopped abruptly, flushing at the intensity of the gaze that the hardheaded realist, Dr. Lorimer, had fixed on her. He'd think she was cracking up. "Anyway, if you gave me this assignment expecting I'd do an exposé or hold them up to fun . . ."

He shook his head. "I wanted a serious article, and that's what you've given me. An excellent job. I only have one bone to pick with you. You didn't give my friend Harper fair play. His account is buried in the very end of the story, and it's only a few lines at that."

"He's been busy." Trudy looked down at her desk as she mumbled the explanation. "The family's been upset since his nephew was hurt."

"I suppose." The professor's voice allowed grudging acceptance of the excuse. "But that doesn't explain mistakes in fact. That's one thing I simply won't allow, Miss McClung."

Trudy wondered how long she would have to be acquainted with the elderly professor before he called her by her first name. It would probably never happened. "Errors?" she asked, ready to defend herself. "I'm careful in my research, Dr. Lorimer."

"Careful?" His voice was glacial, and Trudy sensed the glances of nearby students. They were undoubtedly getting a real kick out of seeing the young woman who usually called them on the carpet getting her turn at being scolded. He leafed through the pages hurriedly, indicating a line near the close of the article with an indignant finger. "What do you call that?"

Puzzled, she took the sheet from him and reread her own words. It wasn't anything to get very excited about, just the part about Jeremy Harper describing his failed interest in football as a step toward his decision to become a minister.

"You don't come right out and say it, Miss McClung, but you suggest that Harper went into the ministry because he couldn't make it in football."

"It was the impression I got," Trudy retorted sharply, "from Dr. Harper himself."

"Then you should check your impressions against the record books." The professor was at his nastiest. "Read a few old newspaper accounts. They're easily located. Jeremy Harper got plenty of attention from this very publication in his student days."

"I knew he'd played college football," Trudy tried to explain, but he wasn't in the mood for interruptions. He turned around, making the whole newsroom his audience.

"Mr. Granbury." He leveled an accusing finger

at Steven, and the blond boy lifted his head abruptly.

"Yes, sir." Steven might have been a military cadet responding to a general.

"Your uncle was a rather successful football player at one time, wasn't he?"

Steven glanced around as though embarrassed. Personally, Trudy wished she could drop quietly through the floor. How was she going to maintain her authority over these students when Dr. Lorimer treated her like this in front of them?

"I asked you a question, Mr. Granbury."

"Uncle Jerry played football here," Steven admitted. "He was good, people tell me. I was only a kid then, so I wouldn't know for sure."

"I was on staff here at the time," Dr. Lorimer contributed. He turned to look further up the long room. "Sports editor!"

Nobody answered. Finally a bespectacled young man half raised one hand. "The editor's over at practice," he said, "but I'm the assistant."

Dr. Lorimer glared at him. "Know your stuff?"

"I . . . I . . . hope so," the boy answered.

"Really, Dr. Lorimer." Indignantly, Trudy tugged at his arm. This was getting out of hand; he was terrorizing her staff.

He pulled away without noticing her attempt at reproof, still directing his attention toward the young assistant at the sports desk. "Tell me about Jerry Harper," he commanded.

To Trudy's surprise the boy sat straighter, and

107

a gleam sparked in his eyes. She knew why he was on the sports desk; he was in love with his subject. "College or pro career?" he asked, suddenly sure of himself.

"Start with college," Dr. Lorimer ordered approvingly, "then work on from there."

"Outstanding fullback," the boy intoned with the air of a TV sports announcer. "Jerry Harper played for Mansfield three years, though he had to sit out part of the first year with a knee injury. He was named all-American two years in a row."

"All-American?" Trudy spoke the question weakly. Slight though her knowledge of the sport was, she knew enough to be impressed.

The boy nodded. "The Associated Press listing," he informed her. "He was a number one draft pick the year he finished college, and the Cowboys chose him in the first round. He went on to play . . ."

"The Cowboys," Trudy murmured. It wasn't a question, but Dr. Lorimer gazed pityingly at her.

"The Dallas Cowboys," he said. He nodded approvingly at the young man who'd supplied the information. "You may just go far, my friend," he said, then scowled as though fearful all the praise would go to the youngster's head. "But only if you work hard and never let up for a moment."

Dr. Lorimer turned his attention back to Trudy, and she could feel the newsroom staff relax and the busy clatter of normal activity resume. He thrust the article into her hands.

"After an outstanding rookie year with the Cowboys, Harper resigned from football. He didn't make any explanations or excuses that I've heard. But after about a year, he was reported as attending a school down in Texas, studying for the ministry. But the one thing you can be sure of is that he didn't give up football because he failed."

"I'll correct the article," Trudy responded meekly.

"Do that and be quick about it. Deadline's coming up." He turned to leave, calling back over his shoulder. "As soon as you've put this edition to bed, Miss McClung, come into my office. I want to talk to you." He gave one last glance at the busy students. "Bring one of the youngsters." His gaze rested on Steven. "Young Granbury will do."

Without further explanation, he walked out of the newsroom. Trudy didn't have time to wonder what he wanted with the two of them; she had an article to correct before deadline time. She didn't even have time to wonder about this new contribution to the enigma of Jeremy Harper. Why would anyone leave a successful and no doubt lucrative career in professional sports to go into low-paying, relatively unrewarding church work?

She shook her head. No time to think about that now. She began to make her corrections.

The newsroom buzz had simmered to a low conversational hum, and Trudy knew it was safe to leave it in the hands of the student editors. She summoned Steven to her side.

"Dr. Lorimer asked to talk to us in his office," she told him.

His mouth twisted wryly. "What have I done wrong?" he asked in a whisper.

Trudy shrugged. "Might as well go find out and end the agony of suspense," she said with a grin.

They walked down the hall together. The presence of the tall blond boy reminded Trudy of his younger brother, and of his uncle as well, though she tried not to think of him. "How is Phil?"

"Fine. Still a little quiet, but more his old self than he was at first. He gets to go home Monday if he keeps doing okay."

"I'm glad," she said. "He must hate being locked up in a hospital room."

Steven grinned. "Now that he's feeling better, he's making the most of it. He has all the nurses fussing over him, and Mom coming and going. Even Miles can't resist him now that he's sick, and usually *he* has good sense. Only Uncle Jerry doesn't give in."

"Your uncle is one tough guy," Trudy told him, matching the grin. "Though I suspect that underneath he'd like to spoil Phil as much as the rest of us do, but he doesn't think it's good for him."

Steven started to answer, but he didn't get a chance. They had reached the door to Dr.

Lorimer's office. He looked at Trudy. "You knock. I'm scared to."

"Nothing to be scared about," Trudy whispered. "You've heard about the dog who was all bark and no bite? Dr. Lorimer is all bite, which means you know exactly what you're dealing with."

She knocked, and the professor's bass boomed at them. "Come in."

Trudy led the way into the small book-lined office. The two of them stood waiting while Dr. Lorimer continued reading without looking up.

Trudy decided she wouldn't let him intimidate her. Steven was shifting uneasily from foot to foot. She had the rank of graduate assistant, and even though Melissa thought of her job as something other than a real teaching position, it was still her responsibility to look after Steven, who was her student.

"We're here, Dr. Lorimer," she informed him crisply.

"I assumed someone was." He didn't look up. "Either that or the door opened by itself, and ghostly footsteps walked into the room."

Difficult man. Trudy wondered how he'd react if she gave the cluttered contents on the surface of his desk a little shove, scattering papers and books onto the floor. He'd at least have to look up.

She resisted the temptation, turning to her companion. "Steven," she said, "Dr. Lorimer is terribly busy and we wouldn't want to interrupt him, so why don't we go down to the basement,

111

get a soda, and relax for a few minutes. Perhaps by the time we've finished, he'll be available to talk to us."

Finally the professor looked up, regarding her with a cool stare. She could almost feel Steven trembling in his tennis shoes, but she stood her ground bravely.

"You wouldn't dare," Dr. Lorimer told her.

Trudy smiled sweetly.

He nodded, his collar-length gray hair swaying gently with the motion. "She would do it," he told himself sadly. "These young women today!"

"Entirely out of hand, aren't they, sir?" Steven spoke hastily, trying to make a joke. It fell flat as the professor's gaze came to rest on him.

"I admire independent women, Mr. Granbury. Simpering clinging vines are a bore."

Steven was too deflated even to agree, but Trudy couldn't help grinning.

"Something amuses you, Miss McClung." Dr. Lorimer was looking at her again.

In a moment's time she'd come to see him more clearly. "You asked to see us," she reminded him.

Instantly he was all business. "You took what could have been a boring, superficial assignment and made something out of it," he told her, ignoring Steven completely.

It was a genuine compliment, and Trudy flushed with pleasure. "I'm glad you liked it."

He waved one hand dismissingly. "No more

than I expected from a competent professional such as yourself. But now that you've passed that test, I'm going to give you something with more meat to it."

He searched through the contents on top of the cluttered desk until finally he dug out a thick folder. He held it up. "Everyone wants to do investigative reporting these days," he said, "dig into political scandals and all that. Well, I've got one for you, Miss McClung. A real live potential political scandal. Could be a hot potato, so you'd better handle it carefully."

"A political scandal?" Trudy repeated, taking the folder into her hands.

"Possibly. I've gotten some information together for you here. Most of it comes from a Mr. Quinlan, a local businessman."

"Automobile dealer," Steven explained to Trudy. "Very successful."

Dr. Lorimer nodded. "He's leveling some serious charges of political corruption."

Trudy looked from the elderly professor to the young man at her side. "If I were Mr. Quinlan and I wanted to tip the press to a need for investigation, would I go to us?" she wondered aloud.

Dr. Lorimer raised one hand. "A student newspaper," he agreed, "operated by a rather small college. That was what I asked, and he had an answer for me. He said the professional press in this state is tied in with vested interests, that they don't want to discover political corruption . . .

and that he feels we will be able to operate more independently.''

Trudy considered the point. The *Mansfield College Daily* had a long tradition of independence to a degree unusual for a student newspaper. She knew the man seated across the desk from her had fought many battles for that independence. Still . . .

''I know, Miss McClung. Don't disregard any of your doubts. Don't take anyone else's word for anything. Prove the facts for yourself.'' His gaze shifted to Steven. ''That goes for you too, Granbury. You're to assist Miss McClung in her research.''

Steven stammered incoherent thanks at the opportunity, and Trudy, taking the folder, left the office with him. Outside the building, she pulled her sweater more closely against the sharp fall wind. The trees were beginning to look thin and wintry as many-colored leaves began falling to dance in the same wind that made her fasten her sweater more tightly. Trudy felt the familiar feeling of adrenaline pumping through her veins at the thought that here at last was a real assignment, one that would call for all her skills.

''Maybe we can have dinner together tonight,'' Steven suggested. ''And go over our game plan?''

''Game plan?'' Trudy asked, half-distracted.

''We need to plan our strategy,'' he reminded her impatiently. ''Figure out how we're going to look into this political corruption charge.''

They walked down the sidewalk that bordered

the college campus. On the other side of the street were big old houses, fading mansions now split up into apartments for students. Trudy eyed them uneasily.

"We could go over to the student center and eat while we make our plans," she agreed, uncomfortably aware of what she'd been told about Steven's crush on her. She didn't want their working together to create a real problem.

"That'd be great," he agreed heartily.

Trudy's eyes fixed on a small sign in a yard up the street. As they drew closer she was able to read the words.

MILES GRANBURY FOR STATE SENATE.

She'd forgotten that the stepfather of her new assistant was in politics himself. She glanced uneasily at Steven. Surely Dr. Lorimer would never have assigned Steven to this task if he'd thought the senior Granbury was involved.

Her mouth set with sudden grimness. Why else would a beginning and unproven journalism student be given such a plum as this assignment? Dr. Lorimer never overlooked anything.

She opened the folder to glance at the first page. It was a brief summary of charges made by the businessman. It suggested that various individuals in responsible positions in state government had been involved in a massive kickback scheme, funneling public money into their own pockets.

115

"I can hardly wait to really get into this," Steven told her eagerly.

Trudy tried to smile. She only hoped he wasn't going to regret being given this assignment.

Chapter Eight

Dinner at the cafeteria turned out to be less of an ordeal than she'd imagined. Stimulated by the thought of the assignment, Steven was all business.

Trudy mapped out a full day of routine research for him. It would mean that Saturday would only be another working day, but he didn't protest. He was as eager to get going as a thoroughbred at the beginning of the Kentucky Derby.

She hid her misgivings from him, but did remind him that the assignment was confidential and that he shouldn't discuss it even with the members of his family. She drew a quick breath of relief when he nodded, not seeming to recognize that there was any particular reason why any member of his family should be kept in the dark.

They were down to the chocolate pudding and the last of their plans when Steven looked past Trudy to wave. "There's Uncle Jerry," he said. Before Trudy could stop him, the wave had turned into a motioning gesture. He was inviting his uncle to join them.

Trudy told herself that if her heart did beat faster as the tall, rugged-faced man approached them, it was only because of her unwillingness to see him again. He had professed his love for her. The best thing she could do, since she couldn't return the feeling, was to avoid him.

"Trudy," he said. "Steven."

It was the first time she'd seen him really ill at ease. For an instant she couldn't imagine what the trouble was; then she understood. He thought she and Steven were here together.

They *were* here together. But not the way he thought.

She started to explain, looking at Steven. But he put his hand possessively on Trudy's, looking proudly up at his uncle. "Join us," he invited. "We're just having dessert."

Trudy thought Jeremy's apologetic refusal of the invitation rang with something less than full sincerity. He explained he was meeting a colleague who hadn't arrived yet but was due at any minute. Before he left, his eyes rested on Trudy. "You'll be happy to know I found that chain for Mike," he told her. "Both he and Blackie are in good shape."

"That's great," Trudy answered, genuinely

pleased at the news. She meant to drop by for a visit with Mike herself one day and see if there was anything she could do to help the youngster.

"What was that all about?" Steven questioned as they finished the last of their dessert and prepared to leave. Trudy began a brief explanation of the meeting with his brother's friend.

As they left the cafeteria, Trudy couldn't resist glancing back to the corner where Jeremy sat. His friend hadn't arrived. He still sat alone, a newspaper unfolded in front of his dinner tray.

It was late the next morning before Trudy realized that she'd forgotten to set her clock the previous evening and the alarm hadn't gone off. When she got up, she discovered it was nearly ten. She hadn't slept so late in years.

The stack of papers on her little desk was evidence that the previous night's work had extended into the early hours of the morning. She'd earned a little extra sleep.

She went over to pull a curtain aside and look out the window. She grimaced at what she saw—a gray rainy day.

She was in no hurry to get outside, and she lingered in her steamy bath liberally laced with scented bath oil, luxuriating in the warmth and the delicate floral scent. She rested her head against the rim of the tub and allowed her body to float sensuously in the soothing liquid. The ringing of the phone startled her from a drowsy reverie, and she reached for the towel, but then drew her hand back.

It was probably her mother again. Who else would be calling her on a Saturday morning?

She let it ring, her body tense until the caller finally gave up and the room was silent again. But the mood of the bath was spoiled, and moments later she stepped out to towel herself dry. She put on a warm robe and went to look out the window again, hoping for a change in the weather. But it was still rainy and gray.

Trudy resolved that in the future she would keep food in her room for such emergencies, but this morning she had no choice but to dress and go out if she wanted anything more than a cup of instant coffee. As a token shield against the chill, colorless day, she selected a warm pink wool dress that would never have done for school because it made her look like a cuddly little co-ed instead of the autocratic controller of the newsroom.

She stepped into her usual high heels, but instead of taking time to tuck her hair into its neat little bun at the back of her head, she hurriedly brushed it into a dusky cloud. Who cared if she looked like a schoolgirl today? Nobody was going to notice as she dashed up to the campus corner for something to eat.

She slipped on her old vinyl raincoat with its protective hood and went out into the hall. Mrs. Larson was coming briskly up the stairs.

"I'm afraid you had another call, Trudy," the elderly woman told her. "That woman again."

"I'm sorry she has your number, Mrs. Larson. It's bad enough that she keeps bothering me."

Mrs. Larson shook her head. "It's not that I mind. She never calls more than once or twice a day, and I'm used to taking calls for the girls who live here. You're the only one with her own phone. But she shouldn't keep troubling you this way, saying she's your mother. There must be something wrong with the woman."

Trudy hesitated uneasily. Mrs. Larson was being bothered with calls. She deserved an explanation.

"She is my mother, Mrs. Larson."

The woman's chubby, kindly face looked troubled. "But you told me . . ."

"I told you she wasn't. That's because I feel she isn't my mother in any sense that counts. She abandoned me when I was a little girl, and I was raised in foster homes and institutions."

"And you never saw her in all that time until now?" Mrs. Larson's eyes were wide with amazement.

Trudy shook her head grimly. This was a story she never told anyone. But Mrs. Larson might be able to deal more firmly with her mother if she knew the facts. "She showed up now and then through the years. She'd take me home with her, make all sorts of promises." Trudy hesitated, aware of the bitterness in her tone. She finished more casually. "You might say she came and went. But that's why I feel like the couple I lived with during my junior and senior years at high school were more my parents, even though they were only providing a foster home. I still write to them regularly."

"Oh, my." Mrs. Larson looked distressed. "Still, dear, she *is* your mother."

Trudy didn't want to hear any more about it. "I tell people my mother is dead," she said. She resumed her walk down the stairs and out of the house, stumbling on the slick steps that led from the wide porch to the ground. Strong hands steadied her.

She looked up. "Jeremy," she said.

He smiled down at her. "Fancy meeting you here."

She was too shaken to protest as he took her hand and led her through the rain to his car. She would get him to drop her on the campus corner; it would save a walk in the rain.

"You were looking for me?" she asked as he started the car.

He looked approvingly at her. She wondered what he could find to like in the worn-out old raincoat. She unbuttoned it so that the pink dress showed, and pushed back the hood that covered her hair.

"I called, but nobody answered, so I thought I'd drop by and see if I could get Mrs. Larson to help me locate you."

"You can drop me at the corner," Trudy said, pointing. She watched as they approached, then drove right by the indicated corner. "I wanted to get out there," she wailed.

"Nope," he told her with a grin. "I'm kidnapping you."

"Kidnapping me?" she asked, frowning at him.

"It's the only way I can get you away from work," he explained. "And I promise to return you by the end of the day so you can put that pretty little nose of yours right back into a book."

"I can't take the whole day off," Trudy protested. "I have a tremendous amount of work to do today, and I was just going out to get something to eat before I started."

"We'll stop on the road and have lunch," he assured her, glancing at his wristwatch. "We have plenty of time."

"Plenty of time for what?" Trudy questioned suspiciously, taking note for the first time of how he looked. He was dressed much as he'd been that day when she'd been so astonished to see him standing in the pulpit of the McFarlin Church. Instead of jeans and a casual sports shirt, he was wearing a dark suit and conservative tie, his unruly golden hair smoothed into a semblance of order. But his smile was as challenging as ever, and his eyes twinkled.

"We're going to a wedding."

"Whose?" Trudy asked suspiciously.

He grinned. "Not ours, this time."

Trudy found herself blushing for no reason at all. She tried to ignore his last remark. "I wasn't invited to a wedding," she pointed out.

"They're friends of mine. You'll be welcome."

"I'm not dressed for a wedding." She looked

down at what showed of the pink wool under her raincoat.

"You look fine for a country wedding. You should wear that color all the time; it matches the pink in your cheeks."

They were already headed out of town, and it was growing warm in the car. Trudy surrendered and pulled off her coat, tossing it to the rear. "A country wedding?" she asked.

He smiled at her. "A little place a couple of hours from here. It's where I grew up. I'd like you to see it."

She finally relaxed enough to return the smile. The day that had seemed so unpleasantly rainy and grim before only made the warmth swirling from the car's heater seem more cozy. It was a nice feeling, as if they were closed in together and there was no one else in the world. "I don't have much choice," she observed demurely, smoothing the pink wool over her legs. "Not if I'm being kidnapped."

The drive through the increasingly wooded countryside seemed to take forever—and to be all too short at the same time. They talked about nothing in particular—the weather; her article in the paper that morning, which she hadn't even seen in print yet; Phil's imminent homecoming.

The rain had slowed to a drippy drizzle that might have seemed unpleasant under other circumstances. But somehow it only reinforced their isolation, the sense of being cut off from the rest of the world.

Even when they stopped for lunch at a little out-of-the-way restaurant, the only other diners were a group of men in western working gear who hovered together in an opposite corner, drinking coffee and talking about their ranch work.

She and Jeremy had bowls of thick homemade soup and crusty fresh-baked bread. They lingered over the meal until Jeremy told her reluctantly that they must go on.

"What's the rush?" She smiled lazily at him, not anxious to share the day with others. "Can't they have this wedding without you?"

He shook his head. "I'm performing the ceremony."

She'd forgotten. She'd actually forgotten. His profession was a barrier between them as effective as an iron gate. They could have no part in each other's lives.

The rain was harder when they stepped back outside, and in spite of the protection of the raincoat, she felt as though she'd stepped into a cold shower. She took her place in the car, sitting as far away from him as she could.

"What's the matter?" he asked, moving the car once again down the little-traveled country road.

She shook her head, closing her eyes to squeeze back the tears. What was the matter with her? Why was she moody like this? Sleeping late wasn't good for her; the whole pace of this day had been awry, from the decision to wear the pink dress to allowing him to carry her off like this. "Nothing's wrong." She strove to keep her voice steady. "I'm only a little tired."

"We'll be there soon," he promised, "and you'll enjoy the wedding. It'll be like nothing you've ever seen—a joyous country wedding, nothing stiff and formal about it."

Trudy didn't want to think about weddings. It was time to change the subject. "Steven tells me Phil is doing well."

He nodded, his eyes on the winding road ahead. "If he doesn't recover quickly, his mother is going to have him spoiled beyond reality."

Trudy didn't know what to say. She agreed, but to say so would seem like a criticism of his sister. "It's odd," she said as a compromise, "because your sister and her husband seem strict enough with Steven."

"It's not Miles. It's Betsy. The boys' father died right after Phil was born, and she's held on to him and tried to overprotect him ever since. It's understandable enough, but I was glad to see Miles enter the picture. He's providing some balance for the boy."

His words gave Trudy some insight into Betsy Granbury's personality. "How hard it must have been for her to lose her husband. That's one of the difficult things about having a good marriage; it must be tragic when it ends."

He shook his head. "It wasn't a good marriage. Betsy ran away with Simon when she was only seventeen. It broke our parents' hearts to see the way he treated her and Steven. But she was stubborn; she wouldn't admit her marriage was a failure."

Trudy was shocked. In spite of her envy of the Granburys, it had been nice to believe in an illusion of perfect family life, interrupted only by such natural events as death. But for Betsy Granbury to have had a miserable first marriage . . .

"I suppose that's why the boys are called by their stepfather's name," she said hesitantly.

"He's the only real father Phil has known," Jeremy confirmed. Suddenly he glanced across at her. It was almost as though he'd touched her.

"This isn't a day to think of failed marriages," he reminded her. "Look happy again so that I'll know I haven't spoiled your afternoon by telling you of Betsy's troubles."

Trudy couldn't respond immediately. Her mind was still back with the Granburys.

"We're there." Jeremy's announcement jarred across her consciousness, and she looked up to see a small white frame church, set at a country crossroads. The building itself was unpretentious, but its setting, amid huge old trees and pastures that stretched into the distance where black and white cows grazed, gave it a natural beauty of its own.

"You grew up here?" she asked, hardly able to believe it. This rural background contrasted sharply with the dignified beauty of Seven Oaks, and even with the stately church he pastored in a college town.

"Sure did." A couple of cars and a florist's van were packed near the front entrance, and he drew his own automobile up alongside them. "My parents were farmers, and I might have followed the same line myself, except I started playing football and kept at it until I was fairly good and colleges started talking scholarships.''

"I've heard you were more than fairly good," Trudy told him.

He grinned. "That was a long time ago. Anyway, let's go in and meet everybody. The groom is an old friend of mine. He and I used to go fishing together when we were about ten."

She followed him through the rain and dampness toward the small church. " 'Happy is the bride the sun shines on,' " she quoted cynically into the dismal day.

"What did you say?" he asked, stopping to look down at her.

"Nothing." Trudy pulled her raincoat more closely about her and walked quickly toward the front door. No use standing around chatting in the rain. It was still afternoon, but already the day was darkening. She didn't like to imagine how depressing this weather must be to a woman who hoped her wedding day would be a beautiful day to remember for the rest of her life.

When they stepped inside, she saw two men and a woman standing near the front of the church, watching as a couple of other people arranged baskets of flowers and constructed a floral arch.

"Jerry!" the younger of the two men yelled out at the sight of them, and he came racing down the aisle. Trudy watched as the two men indulged in the hearty handshaking, backslapping ritual with

128

which some men show affection.

Finally Jerry stepped back. "Now, Owen," he said. "It's way too early for the groom to be at the church."

The man addressed as Owen grinned so widely that Trudy thought his slender face would split. He was nearly as tall as Jeremy, but slender to the point of emaciation, with the lean body and weathered complexion of an outdoorsman.

"I couldn't stand staying around the house by myself," he confessed. "I would've had a nervous breakdown. So I came on over to bother the preacher and the florist people."

"Trudy." Jeremy suddenly circled her shoulders possessively with one arm. "I want you to meet one of my oldest friends, Owen Hackett."

Trudy found her hand being pumped in a hearty handshake. "Glad to meet you, Trudy," he said. "Never knew of Jerry to come visiting with a girl before. Does this mean he's about to follow my example? He always was a copycat!"

It took a moment for Trudy to figure out what he was talking about; then she glanced to the front of the church, where preparations were being made for the wedding. She wished there were some way to keep from blushing, but she knew her face must have been as red as a summer rose.

Jeremy laughed. "You'll scare her off talking that way, Owen," he said. "I was trying to slip up on the thing gradually."

Gradually! Trudy couldn't help remembering the day at Seven Oaks when, after only a brief acquaintance, he'd told her he loved her and meant to marry her.

He grinned when she looked at him, as though guessing what she was thinking.

Trudy hadn't realized that the older couple had joined them until a soft, sweet voice spoke. "You might let me tell her a thing or two about being a minister's wife before she takes the plunge, Jerry. It's only fair she be forewarned."

Jeremy turned around to be wrapped in a warm hug by a silver-haired woman in her seventies, who was accompanied by a keen-eyed elderly man.

"Come on, Rachel," the man protested. "You mustn't make her think it's that bad."

They both smiled as though remembering. In spite of their years, they seemed young to Trudy. It was something about their eyes.

Trudy was introduced to Jim and Rachel McDonald. He had been pastor of this tiny church for many years.

The sounds of cars driving up outside reached their ears, and Owen began to look more nervous than ever, if such a thing was possible. Jeremy and the Reverend McDonald took him in hand. It was time for him to go into seclusion in one of the little rooms back of the choir seats. But before he left, Jeremy looked anxiously at Trudy.

Mrs. McDonald took the younger woman's arm. "Jim and I will look after your young lady. She'll sit with us."

Trudy was glad to have company in this crowd

130

of strangers, and she could see already that in spite of the rain, it was going to be quite a crowd. Whole families came in to find seats on either the bride or groom's side. As Jeremy had told her, there was little that was formal about this occasion. People laughed and joked as though at a party, leaning across pews to exchange the latest news.

Nearly everyone that came in stopped by to exchange the greetings with the woman at her side, and Trudy was duly introduced as Jeremy Harper's friend. The word seemed to have a special significance, and these people who had known Jeremy since he was a little boy looked at her with curiosity.

It was just as well she'd never be coming back to this place. Jeremy's teasing remarks to his friends when they arrived were being taken like an announcement of an engagement.

Mrs. McDonald reached across to pat her hand. "Don't let what we said scare you, my dear. Being a minister's wife has great rewards."

Trudy smiled uncomfortably. "Jeremy and I haven't known each other very long," she said, glad to be able to get the real situation out in the open. "And we're not at all serious about each other."

Mrs. McDonald hardly seemed to hear. "I used to worry about Jerry. He got wild after his parents died . . . only six months apart. It was sad. And he was terribly concerned about his sister. Then, when he went away to college, it was like he forgot everything he was ever taught." She shook her head. "I can tell you, I didn't care for the girls he ran around with then."

Trudy was embarrassed. Mrs. McDonald undoubtedly thought she was someone like Melissa Reven, a woman who attended church regularly and sang in the choir. The truth was she couldn't even carry a tune.

Abruptly Mrs. McDonald put a hand to her own mouth. "Just listen to me running on. Jim would give me a good talking-to if he heard me telling you about Jeremy's past and other girls he went out with. I keep hoping I'll acquire some tact."

So Jeremy had a past. Trudy was torn between amusement and dismay.

Mrs. McDonald was still talking. "People expect so much from a minister's wife. Her house must always shine, her children be perfectly behaved, and yet she always has to be at church every time the doors open, and leading many of the activities. You're supposed to be friendly, but somehow a little better than everyone else." She paused to laugh. "I don't know how I managed, because I have so many faults, but somehow Jim never seemed to really mind. He said I didn't have to be perfect, that I was exactly the wife he wanted."

Trudy didn't get a chance to answer because the Reverend McDonald joined them to sit down by his wife, and seconds later the pianist took her place. With the first strains of music, the conversation in the pews died and people leaned forward expectantly.

When the music rose joyously, Trudy turned with the others toward the back of the church where the bride and her father were coming up the steps from the basement. Then the white-gowned figure stood poised, hesitating for a heartbeat.

Trudy's first thought was that it was a shame the bride was so plain. Her face was pleasantly rounded but had little claim to beauty, and her figure was too plump to be made glamorous even by the beauty of a traditional wedding gown.

Then the bride and her father moved down the aisle and toward them. Trudy's eyes were fixed on them until they moved past her; then she turned around.

While she'd been watching the back, Jeremy, Owen and the young man who was best man had slipped into place at the front of the church. Trudy caught one glimpse of Owen's nervous, enraptured face as he watched his bride come down the aisle, and she realized one thing: the bride might not be beautiful in her eyes or in those of the other onlookers, but to Owen Hackett she was the loveliest woman ever born.

Something like a shiver ran through Trudy's body. What nonsense was she thinking?

"What's wrong, dear?" Mrs. McDonald bent close to whisper.

"Nothing," Trudy whispered back. Nothing was wrong except that she was losing her mind.

For the rest of the brief ceremony, she watched

Jeremy, listened to the way in which he spoke the simple but dramatic words of the marriage service. Radiance was cast by flickering candles in the darkness of the early evening. Even the rain couldn't dim this wedding. It didn't need the sun to shine on it.

Trudy had a feeling that something special, something almost holy was happening that she had no part in. She didn't want to be caught up in this. She wanted to jump up and run down the aisle.

Marriage was not something to be taken lightly, to be entered into casually, nor as easily ended. Marriage was . . . awesome.

She heard Jeremy pronounce the couple united, was dimly aware of their kiss and the triumphant march back down the aisle. But her eyes were on Jeremy's face.

"Dear God," she spoke in silent confession. "You know how much I love him."

Chapter Nine

The rain that danced incessantly in the headlights was heavier now, and Trudy was glad they were almost home. She was tired and depressed. She felt almost as though something terrible had happened.

She couldn't be in love with Jeremy Harper. And yet she had no choice about the way she felt.

"You've been awfully quiet," he told her. "You've hardly said a word on the whole trip back. Mad because I made you go along?"

She shook her head, feeling ridiculously close to tears. "It was a lovely wedding and I liked your friends." True enough, but she wished she'd never witnessed the wedding, never met his friends, never come to this realization of feelings for him that would haunt her for the rest of her life.

Not that the way she felt would change anything; she couldn't let it.

"It felt right having you there," he told her. "I've never had anybody I wanted to take home to meet the people who've been close to me since I was a child."

She watched the dancing rain and didn't look at him. "You have your family," she pointed out, "and multitudes of friends. I don't have a part in your life." She didn't have to look around to know he was shaking his head.

"It's not the same. Everybody needs someone special, someone who's worth fighting the whole world for."

She shivered. Even the pink wool dress wasn't enough to keep her warm. He loved her—or so he said. And she loved him. Equal sides of an equation. But it wasn't that simple.

"You're not answering me." His voice was gentle.

"I didn't hear a question."

"I may not have come right out and said it, but you know what the question is." His voice sharpened as though impatient with her pretense.

It was pretense. She knew exactly what he was saying.

"Mrs. McDonald said you had a past." She didn't know why she said it; she hadn't meant to.

He laughed. "Everyone does. But she's right; I'm not particularly proud of the person I was. In fact, I'm not always proud of myself now, though I do my best."

"I thought you were practically ready for a halo," Trudy confessed in a woebegone little girl's voice. "After all, you are a minister."

The lights of town glimmered ahead of them already, but suddenly he swung the car over to the grassy shoulder of the road and turned the engine off. He reached for her, taking hold of her shoulders. "Look at me," he commanded in a rough-edged voice. "You haven't really looked at me in two hours."

Defiantly Trudy stared up at him. The temper she'd barely seen, but which he confessed as a serious problem, burned in his eyes. She started to speak, but his mouth closed on hers and they kissed. Their feelings for each other flowed in a warm current between them for a long moment; then she made herself pull away.

She stared up at him, knowing how hard the realization she'd had during the wedding would make this moment. She had to keep it light.

"Pastors aren't allowed to have feelings?" His voice was still angry. "They aren't allowed to fall in love?"

Trudy turned to him. His face was white, strained with emotion. She couldn't pretend to make fun of the way he felt. "I had some idea . . . I thought somehow that you were supposed to be slightly above human emotions, living on a higher plane."

"My belief is intertwined with every aspect of my life. It isn't something set aside for Sunday and the church. And it is my conviction that love between a man and a woman is one of the greatest of God's earthly gifts."

Trudy closed her eyes. That was the way she'd felt there in the little country church, as though Owen and his bride were especially blessed. She opened her eyes. "Not many people feel that way these days."

Neither of them spoke for a moment. Finally he broke the silence. "Is it Steven?" he asked. "If you tell me that you care for someone else, I'll leave you alone."

She opened her mouth to speak the lie that would free her from him, but the words wouldn't come. "Take me home," was the only message she could choke out.

He started the car and they drove on without talking, reaching town within a few minutes. Silently he brought the car to a stop in front of her rooming house.

It was still raining, but Trudy's fumbling as she tried to put her raincoat back on was more a stalling device than anything else. She couldn't bear to leave him like this. He looked so hurt. She wanted him to put his strong arms around her again so she could hide her face against his jacket and feel warm and safe and secure from the world.

"Trudy," he said.

She stared out the window at the face of her house. Then, impulsively, she turned toward him, suddenly wildly happy, ready to fling the caution and restraint of years aside and tell him exactly how much, how very much she loved him.

But before she could speak, a bright orange taxi drew up in front of them to allow a slender woman to step out and unfurl her umbrella. She stared anxiously at the rooming house.

It was her mother.

Trudy felt as though all the cold of this rainy day had been dumped on her spirits. "I'd better get inside," she told him in a lifeless voice. "I've got work to do."

"But, Trudy!" He wanted to stop her, but she wouldn't listen. She pushed the door open and stepped out into the rain.

"You haven't convinced me yet," he called after her. "I haven't given up."

Trudy ran toward the front steps, not even being careful about where she placed her high-heeled shoes on the slippery walk. She brushed past her mother, who was just climbing onto the porch.

"Trudy! I've got to talk to you." Her mother grabbed hold of the sleeve of Trudy's raincoat. Trudy tried to free herself, but the grip wasn't released.

"I've called and I've come by, and you won't listen to me. We've got to talk. It's important to me."

"But not to me," Trudy responded coldly. The hood of her coat had slipped back, and a steady drip of water was draining down the back of her neck. She was conscious that Jeremy's car still sat unmoving in front of the house and that he was probably watching this unpleasant little scene.

"I won't leave until you talk to me." Her mother's strength was usually a thin shell. It only took a little resistance to make her back down, but today Trudy sensed a desperate kind of stubbornness.

"We could go up to my room," she finally agreed. "But I can only give you ten minutes."

"That's enough." Pathetic eagerness was in the other woman's voice, and Trudy stiffened herself against it. Her mother was good at making people feel sorry for her.

Tired and depressed, she led the way up the stairs and fumbled with the key that unlocked the door. The room with its unmade bed seemed cheerless. Trudy flicked on the light and drew the curtains against the outside world.

She hung her raincoat and her mother's umbrella in the tiled bathroom, where they could drip without doing any permanent damage. Then she turned to look at the woman who was her mother. She'd agreed to put herself through this ordeal one last time. She set her jaw grimly. Perhaps the best way would be to pretend she was entertaining a stranger. In a way it was true.

"I can make instant coffee," she said, speaking as though to a casual guest. "Would you like a cup?"

"That would be nice," her mother responded in kind.

Trudy went over to her desk, extracting coffee, powdered creamer, sugar, cups and spoon from the bottom drawer. She plugged in the hot plate and placed a small kettle of water on it.

"You can sit down." She indicated the one comfortable chair, seating herself in the unpadded wooden chair that went with her desk.

Her mother sat down also, staring wordlessly at Trudy. She betrayed her nervousness only by the way she kept rubbing one hand over the upholstered arm of the chair. "I've been wanting to have a good talk with you for a long time."

"Then talk." Trudy knew she might as well be blunt. This woman had earned nothing more from her.

The brown-haired woman nodded. "I've done a lot of things wrong," she began. "I've done a good job of messing up your life and mine, but I've always loved you, darling. Always."

Trudy covered her eyes wearily with one hand. The same old story again and again. "I've always thought you could judge true feelings by what people did, not what they said. Your actions said you didn't love me."

"I was so young when I married your father, when you were born." Her mother laughed, a short bitter laugh. "I thought I was going to live happily ever after, the way they do in stories. Then when he was killed in the accident at work . . . It's still as though it just happened, Trudy, like they've just come to tell me."

Trudy didn't know what she was expected to say. She'd been less than a year old when her father died. Anyway, she was firmly convinced that anyone who had messed up her life as much as her mother had would have found some excuse for it.

She got to her feet to make the coffee. "Sugar and cream?" she asked.

Her mother shook her head. "I like it black."

Trudy passed the cup, added powdered creamer to her cup, and stirred until the liquid was golden brown. Maybe the hot drink would drive away the chill of the day. She sipped it slowly.

Her mother put her cup down. "A man has asked me to marry him," she said. "A fine man."

Trudy wasn't surprised. It was strange, when you heard all the time how few available men there were compared to the number of available women her mother's age, how she always seemed to come up with one. Trudy looked curiously at the other woman, trying to gauge from the slightly fading beauty what it was that drew men to her.

"What is this?" she asked. "The fifth time?"

Her mother sat upright with an offended air. "I've only been married three times, and as I've just said, I was terribly young when I married your father."

Trudy smiled unpleasantly. "I suppose I'm only remembering the times when you didn't marry them."

Her mother reached for her cup again, her hand shaking so that the coffee spilled over the edge of the cup, and Trudy had to get a paper towel to clean it before it soaked into the rug.

"I'm sorry," she said, when she sat back down again. "It's no business of mine how you live. I hope you and this new man are happy together."

The phone rang, and Trudy welcomed the interruption to a painful conversation. She didn't like the things she was saying. She wanted to be remote from her mother's life, not little-girl hurt.

Betsy Granbury's voice sounded in her ear. "I've been at the hospital visiting Phil."

"He's not feeling worse?" Trudy felt a sudden sharp fear.

"No, he's coming along fine. But he gets bored and wants visitors constantly. Jerry's with him now, and I thought you might meet me at Christopher's. We could have dinner together if you haven't eaten."

"I haven't had dinner," Trudy admitted, her thoughts scattered. Why would Betsy Granbury want to have dinner with her? The answer came as quickly as the question. She was worried about Steven and his infatuation. It certainly should be no problem to reassure her.

"In about half an hour then, at Christopher's?" the silvery voice sounded again.

Trudy agreed, then hung up. This would give her an excuse to get away from her mother, who had already overstayed the agreed-upon ten minutes. "I'm going to have to go out. I'm meeting someone for dinner."

Her mother stared at her without comprehension. "He has children," she said.

Trudy blinked. "Who has children?"

"The man who wants me to marry him. He has a boy who's seven and a girl who will be fourteen in January. He says a girl that age needs a mother to guide her. It's a difficult age."

"I know," Trudy answered. "When I was fourteen, I was living in a cottage at a children's home. The housemother tried to be understanding, but she had ten girls to look after."

"I love him, Trudy." Tears stood in the brown eyes. "And he loves me."

Trudy didn't sit down again, but went to the window where she pushed the curtain aside to look out. The rain had finally stopped, but she decided to indulge in a cab to Christopher's nonetheless. She didn't want to face Jeremy's sister all rumpled from walking.

"I can make him happy, Trudy. It's those children I'm worried about, the girl and the boy. It matters so much, and I've messed up with you so badly. But I'm older now, more mature. I've learned through my mistakes. I can be a good mother to them."

Trudy frowned, not wanting to hear any of this. "Why say this to me? What does it have to do with me?"

The woman in the chair got up, setting her coffee cup down carefully on the desk top, and she approached her daughter, one hand outstretched. "Because I failed you. You've got to tell me I have a chance of succeeding now, that it'll be different. Otherwise I can't risk everything with those two children."

Trudy edged away until her back was against the wall. She was so tired. "How can I tell you that, when each time you've showed up in my life, you've told me that from now on things would be different, that you'd fallen in love with someone who would solve all our problems and that we were going to be together and happy again? Haven't you learned that you have to take charge of your own life? It's the same old story you're telling me! You'll never change."

Dorothy Samuels stared at her with wide brown eyes like those of a stricken deer. She started to speak, whispered a word or two, then stopped. Wordlessly, she turned and started toward the door.

"Your umbrella," Trudy called after her. She ran into the bathroom for the object and thrust it into her mother's hands. "It's your life," she urged. "Make your own decisions; do whatever you want. Only leave me out of it."

The other woman nodded blindly, then turned the doorknob and stepped out into the hall. The door closed behind her.

Trudy was hit by an impulse to run after her to offer what comfort she could. Her mother was always like that, a woman in her forties who still needed to be comforted like a child.

She suppressed the impulse. Maybe she'd finally gotten rid of her for good tonight.

Trudy didn't have time to think about it. She couldn't face chic Betsy Granbury in a dress she'd worn all day. She glanced at her watch. Only fifteen minutes left!

There was no time for a bath, but she took one anyway, allowing herself only three minutes in the warm water. Then she dressed quickly in her best pants suit, a trim navy blue, with a wildly printed contrasting blouse in a soft fabric.

She called a cab before doing her hair, and by the time she was ready it was waiting outside.

Christopher's was the fanciest restaurant in Mansfield, Oklahoma. It offered considerably more atmosphere than the corner eating places Trudy frequented when she didn't go to the student-center cafeteria.

Breathlessly she smiled at the young hostess. "I'm meeting someone."

"Mrs. Granbury told me to expect her guest." The young woman smiled and conducted Trudy past a sparkling, lighted fountain and an abundance of fresh greenery to a secluded table. Betsy Granbury smiled at her. "I'm having coffee," she said, "but do have a drink if you prefer."

Trudy shook her head. "Coffee for me too," she told the hostess. She'd gotten no more than a chance to sip at the cup of coffee that was still cooling in her room.

Betsy Granbury didn't look like a woman who'd spent hours in the hospital at her son's bedside. Her lime green dress was simple in style, but even Trudy, who was accustomed to shopping at discount racks at the better department stores, recognized its quality. Her shimmering blond hair was swept up in a style that bore little resemblance to the schoolmarm knot Trudy wore for professional occasions. Soft, carefully controlled wisps of hair framed a patrician face.

"I ordered for us so that we'd have time to talk." Betsy Granbury smiled again. "Christopher's makes a delicious filet of sole. I hope you enjoy it."

Trudy glanced around at the beautiful restaurant. She doubted that anything Christopher's prepared could help but be an improvement over the hearty, rather plain food she usually ate.

"Sounds perfect," she said. She found herself unexpectedly intimidated by the presence of Jeremy Harper's lovely sister. She tried to remember what he'd said about the bad marriage and the other problems in Betsy's life. She hoped that the knowledge of them might make her feel that they were on the same level. But Betsy sat there smiling and looking so composed, making Trudy wish she were somewhere else.

Pretend you're here to interview her, she told herself. You've talked to everyone from the governor to a death-row inmate without feeling this nervous. Was she this nervous because Betsy was Jeremy's sister? She wouldn't allow herself to think about that.

"You wanted to talk to me about something, Mrs. Granbury?" That sounded more like the familiar Trudy who could talk to anybody about anything because it was her job.

"Call me Betsy, because I certainly intend to call you Trudy."

Did the woman never stop smiling? "I think I know what you want to talk to me about, Betsy. It must be about Steven."

"Steven?" The smile finally faded. "Not Steven, unless he's having problems with his college work. But he assures me he's very happy . . . Oh, you mean about his being in love with you?"

Trudy nodded. "I thought you might be concerned about that."

"Dear me, no." The smile broadened until Betsy Granbury was laughing softly. "Steven has to be in love with someone, and I'm sure you understood the nature of his infatuation right from the start. Luckily, at the same time he's in love with you, he's also dating a pretty little redhead from one of the best sororities, and a willowy brunette who is teaching him to golf."

"That puts me in my place," Trudy admitted. "One of a crowd."

"Think of it as a compliment. Steven admires you very much, and as his uncle says, he has excellent taste."

The permanently fixed smile on Betsy Granbury's face melted a little around the edges, but she didn't say anything while Trudy's coffee was served and plates of salad were put in front of them.

She watched the waiter walk away. "It's my brother I'm here to talk about."

Trudy stirred real cream into her coffee. "Your brother?" she asked disbelievingly.

"I didn't realize what the situation was until I talked to Melissa. She told me Jeremy, not Steven, is your real interest."

Trudy waved a hand dismissingly, but Betsy didn't allow her to speak. "Naturally I didn't place a lot of credence in what Melissa said, but when I talked to Jeremy he confirmed it. He admitted he was in love with you." Betsy bent across the table toward Trudy. "I have to make you understand what a disaster this could be for my brother."

Chapter Ten

The conversation was interrupted by the waiter placing food on the table in front of them. It had been many hours since Trudy had eaten, but she didn't even look at her plate.

She'd spent all afternoon reminding herself she couldn't think of marrying Jeremy Harper, but now that his sister was telling her the same thing, she wanted to argue.

The waiter had only moved two steps away from their table when she spoke. "Isn't disaster a rather strong word to use?"

"You don't know my brother as I do. He had lots of girls back in college and in his football career days, but since then . . . there's been no one serious, no one he really cared about. He wants to marry you."

"And you think that would be a disaster?"

Trudy poked at the filet of sole with her fork. It looked delicious, but she knew she couldn't eat a single mouthful. "Am I so awful?"

"Oh, my dear!" Betsy's fair skin was abruptly tinged with pink, and she reached an apologetic hand across the table. "I didn't mean it that way. You're an attractive and charming woman, but I've talked to Steven and I've talked to Jeremy. Neither of them can assure me that you're not the angry, troubled woman I think you are."

"You mean I don't speak the right language?" Trudy asked bitterly. "You want him to marry someone like Melissa, who knows all the right things to say."

Betsy looked down at her food. She wasn't eating either. "I made a mistake in my first marriage," she confessed. "I don't often admit that to people, but I care a great deal about my brother, and I don't want an infatuation to ruin his life."

Trudy stared defiantly across the table. "You want him to play it safe like you did in your second marriage and choose someone proper and reliable who offers security, loyalty, and other good-scout qualities."

Betsy Granbury's face was more than just tinged with pink now; it burned an angry red. "You have no right to say such things to me."

Trudy's eyebrows rose. "But you have a right to warn me away from Jeremy?"

Their eyes met. Finally Betsy spoke. "Miles is a wonderful person. I've come to love him."

"I'm sure he's properly grateful."

"It isn't like that." Betsy looked appealingly at her. "You can't understand what it's like between my husband and me."

Trudy pushed her chair back. "And you can't understand how Jeremy and I feel, how all the security and . . . and proper behavior in the world don't seem to hold a candle to the way we feel about each other." She stumbled to her feet. "I'm not hungry anymore. Thank you for the lovely dinner, but I have to get home."

Betsy Granbury got to her feet, and a waiter hurried toward them, obviously distressed that the beautiful meal was going untouched. Trudy walked rapidly from the restaurant, breaking into a run as she got outside. It was raining again and starting to get cold, but she couldn't stand around waiting for a taxi.

She was about half a block up the street when she heard a car come to a stop nearby and a familiar voice called out to her. "Need a lift?"

"Not from you, Jeremy Harper," she shouted back, refusing to turn around. She doubted he'd believe her face was wet because of the rain, and not because she was crying.

She heard the car door open and the sound of footsteps running toward her. He grabbed her shoulder and swung her around. "Don't be foolish. You don't even have a coat and you're getting soaked."

She had little choice but to allow him to lead her back to the little car. Sullenly she took her place in the passenger seat.

"Everything okay?" he asked.

"I'm fine." She wasn't fine. Her hair was sodden and the blue suit was heavy with moisture. But in spite of that, she would rather have walked the whole way in the rain than ride with him.

"I've been visiting Phil," he said, "and was on my way home when I happened to see you running the hundred-yard dash in the rain."

She was in no mood for humor. "How fortunate," she answered miserably.

"What's wrong, Trudy?" he asked, his voice suddenly gentle. "Does it have something to do with that woman I saw you talking to when you got out of the car earlier this evening? You looked so upset when you saw her."

Trudy had never liked to talk about her mother, but this was a good excuse for her obviously distraught state. "That's it," she said. "I was upset about the meeting and went out for a walk to think about it and got caught in the rain."

"Anything I can help you with?"

She shook her head. "Not unless you can rewrite my childhood. That was my mother you saw at the house this evening."

"Your mother? You said she was dead."

"That's what I tell people. Actually she dumped me. That's an embarrassing thing to confess, isn't it? That you weren't pretty enough or interesting enough for your own mother to want you? Anyway, she took off when I was a little girl, leaving me with anyone willing to take responsibility. I wouldn't mind that so much, but she has a way of showing up now and then to tell me how she's changed and wants to start all over again. I used to believe her, but now that I'm over twenty-one, I don't believe in fairy tales anymore."

The words tumbled out without design. Trudy never talked about her mother, and yet she was rattling on and on about her. She knew why. It was because suddenly the problem of her mother was nothing compared to the problem of the way she felt about the man at her side.

"Pull over to the side of the street," she suddenly commanded.

He looked at her curiously, but did as she asked. When the car was fully stopped, she moved over next to him. "Kiss me," she demanded.

An odd little smile captured his mouth as he looked quizzically down at her. "What?"

She placed her lips firmly against his, pressing fiercely until he responded. The kiss was long, and he cooperated so fully that when she pulled away she had to gasp for breath.

She moved away then, knowing why she'd been compelled to demand the kiss. It was good-bye. "Take me home," she said. "I've got to get some dry clothes."

He took off his own jacket and wrapped it around her shivering body before starting the car. Heat circulated around her ankles as they drove on, but she couldn't stop shaking.

"Your sister says I'm much too bitter and

angry to make a good wife." She spoke the accusation aloud, not knowing she was going to say it until the words had actually come out.

"You talked to Betsy?"

Trudy nodded, close to tears.

They were at her house now, and he parked the car in front before speaking. "Betsy had no right to get involved." He sounded terribly angry, but he hadn't denied what his sister had said. "Darling." He reached out to put an arm around her, but she sat stiff and unyielding in his embrace. "I pray always that you will find some peace in your life."

The tears and the shaking stopped. Enraged, Trudy pulled away from him. "I don't need your prayers," she informed him. "I like my life the way it is. And you can tell your sister I wouldn't marry you if . . . if . . . that the life of a minister's wife is the least desirable I can imagine." She reached for the door handle and was halfway out of the car before he grabbed her arm.

Even through her anger, she could see the deep hurt in his eyes. "Don't be offended by my prayers," he told her. "You'll always be in them because I'll always love you, even if you never let me see you again."

It was madness. He'd told her of his terrible temper, and yet when she struck out at him with words, he only responded with love and concern. It would have been easier if he'd yelled, or tried to hit her.

She stared at him a moment longer, then ran into the house.

The early morning alarm only made Trudy burrow deeper into the covers of her warm bed. Even before she was awake enough to consciously reason why, she knew she didn't want to get up and face the day ahead of her.

The thought of Jeremy was like a throbbing infection that she didn't want to touch. But she turned over and remembered that she had an appointment with Mel Quinlan, the businessman who had complained about political corruption.

She got out of bed, bathed hastily, and dressed. She would have to skip breakfast in order to talk to Mr. Quinlan before her responsibilities at the school began.

She had no choice but to splurge once more on a cab because Quinlan Motors was on the highway outside town. The glass-enclosed automotive showroom was locked, but when she tapped lightly at the door, a man came to let her in.

Mel Quinlan was different from what she'd expected. He looked to be in his mid-fifties, and was good-looking in the polished manner of a television newsman. He welcomed her enthusiastically and showed her to his office. Trudy walked past shiny new automobiles and past a row of office cubicles before they came to the big corner office with its plush chairs and huge desk.

Quinlan sat behind the desk. "I would have thought from the looks of you that they were sending in the second string," he said. "But Gerald Lorimer has assured me you're the best."

Trudy had learned a long time ago not to let personal remarks influence her work. "It does puzzle me, Mr. Quinlan, that you would come to a college newspaper with your charges." It was the point she'd already brought up with Dr. Lorimer, but she wanted to hear Quinlan discuss it.

He shrugged. "Don't sell the *Mansfield College Daily* short. It's a good little paper, well edited and as honest as any newspaper in the state. Besides, some of the others have a certain bias. They wouldn't want to listen to me. But if we get good coverage in the *Daily,* they'll be on the bandwagon soon enough."

"In other words, you're using us to get wider attention throughout Oklahoma."

He grinned, not bothering to deny the charge. "I'm using you; you're using me. You get a hot story when I've already done most of the work."

He went over to the other side of the room, and Trudy watched while he unlocked a large file drawer. From it he removed a box. He set it on the table in front of her and opened it to reveal a thick stack of papers. "Invoices," he said, "statements and other evidence that kickback payments were made."

Trudy picked up the paper on top. It was evidence that a construction company had paid large fees to a county commissioner in order to get the bid on a substantial county project. The county named was Mansfield County.

And Miles Granbury was the commissioner!

Trudy kept her expression carefully impassive. "You'll understand that I'll have to begin my own investigation. I can't simply write a story based on what you have here."

Quinlan's handsome face ruffled with displeasure. "Can't see why not. I've spent months doing my homework."

"I'm sure you have." Trudy's voice was firm. The matter was not negotiable. She would do her own research. "Now if you have no reluctance to parting with this material . . ."

"Copies." He raised one hand. "It's not that I don't trust you, but I wouldn't let the originals out of my hands for any amount of money. Miles Granbury would pay plenty to see they were destroyed."

Granbury again. Trudy picked up the stack of papers. She would have to go back to Dr. Lorimer and ask that Steven be relieved of the assignment. It wasn't fair to expect him to investigate his stepfather.

"I'll go over these documents thoroughly," she said. "And talk with some of the same people you interviewed. Then I'll get back to you."

He nodded, rising to his feet. "Be happy to help you in any way I can, little lady."

Trudy tried not to be offended by his condescending tone. In spite of his good looks, friendly manner, and obviously booming business, she didn't like Mel Quinlan.

It wasn't fair to make such a judgment of a man she'd only know ten minutes, and Trudy recognized why she felt that way. It was because of Phil and Steven and the way they felt about their stepfather. She was on their side.

But a good journalist couldn't afford to take sides.

She forced herself to smile as she asked to use a phone to call a cab. He refused her request, offering instead to drive her into town.

Trudy leaned back in the seat of the luxurious automobile Quinlan drove and pondered what to do next. By the time they got to town she'd already decided. She went straight to Dr. Lorimer's office at the journalism school. The graying professor didn't look surprised to see her.

"I've been out to see Mr. Quinlan." She didn't bother with polite preliminaries. "I haven't gotten a chance to go over the information he's given me, but he's suggesting Miles Granbury is involved."

Dr. Lorimer gazed unblinkingly at her. Obviously the news wasn't a surprise to him. "So?"

"You already knew," she accused.

He shook his head. "I didn't know, but I suspected. Miles Granbury is a big wheel in local politics, and it looks like he's headed for the same role at the state level. Anything going on around here, he'd be likely to be involved."

"But you said Jeremy was your friend."

"Harper would be the last man to ask me to go

159

easy on possible criminal activities just because his brother-in-law was involved." Dr. Lorimer's tone was unusually mild, and Trudy couldn't help wondering what he was up to. "Look," he said. "Quinlan came to me with some apparently well based charges against public officials. That's our job here, isn't it, to keep a look out for the public good and let the people know when those who work for them are taking advantage of that fact to feather their own private nests?"

Trudy had to agree with such an obvious truth. "But you assigned Steven Granbury to assist me, knowing his stepfather might be involved."

"I didn't know."

"Don't quibble," she snapped.

"You certainly are out of sorts today, Miss McClung." His tone was still mild. "Must have gotten up on the wrong side of the bed."

"It was the fact that I had to start off the day talking to that oily character by the name of Mel Quinlan," she informed his coldly.

She knew before he spoke that his patience was suddenly gone. "Let the facts speak for themselves," he told her, his voice crisp. "Personalities don't play a part in a matter like this."

It was what she'd been telling herself, but she didn't like having someone else point it out to her.

"You will take Steven off the assignment?" She made the one last plea.

He shook his head. "Young Granbury can handle it," he said. "Or he has no business in this profession."

160

"But what will it do to him if we find out his stepfather is a . . . a . . ."

"Crook." Dr. Lorimer wasn't one for mincing words. "You're looking at the negative, Miss McClung. Maybe you'll find he's innocent as a babe. Think how Steven will feel to be taking part in the clearing of his stepfather's name."

Trudy had been in reporting too long to be willing to place all her bets on the possibility of a public official's total innocence. "Please take Steven off the assignment," she begged.

Once again Dr. Lorimer shook his head. "No," he said. He picked up a book and began, pointedly, to read, indicating that the discussion was at an end.

Trudy went down the hall to the *Daily* office. Her normal routine was only beginning, but she felt as though she'd already put in a full day's work.

By the time Trudy's shift at supervising the activities of the little newspaper was at an end, Steven was questioning her anxiously about when they were going to get started on their big story. He'd already gained considerable status with his classmates because of the assignment.

Trudy looked at his eager eyes and wished there were some way she could spare him the honor. But Dr. Lorimer was boss.

"I set up an interview for late this afternoon," she finally admitted. "You can go along and take notes."

161

"Great!" Under any other circumstances his enthusiasm would have been contagious. "Who are we talking to?"

"A Mr. Myers." She glanced down at her notebook. "He's a partner in a company that specializes in highway construction."

"Sure. They're building that new highway in the southern part of the county. He and Mr. Quinlan came by the house a couple of times to talk to Dad."

Trudy's heart sank. She wondered how long it would take for Steven to put together the facts. "We might as well go now and get it over with."

Steven drove her to offices in the downtown area. They went inside and Trudy introduced the boy to the businessman by his first name, identifying him only as her assistant. In spite of the meetings Steven had mentioned, he didn't seem to recognize the young man. He was too eager to tell his story.

"Mel Quinlan told me somebody would be contacting me." He concentrated his attention on Trudy. "And I agree with Mel. It's time we let the truth about Granbury come out."

Trudy saw Steven's sudden start, his surprised look. But Mr. Myers was looking at Trudy and couldn't see the boy's face.

"You're saying that Miles Granbury was involved in an illegal kickback scheme during his term of office as county commissioner?" she asked, her voice carefully controlled. She almost wished she'd prepared Steven in some way.

"You bet. He sits up there in that big house in the country with that pretty young wife of his, looking like dirt couldn't touch him. But let me tell you, I had to come across with a bundle to get the contract on that highway I'm building now."

"We'll need specifics," Trudy said, her throat dry. "And proof. You'll understand that we can't publish anything on your word alone, Mr. Myers."

"Sure. Sure. Though I don't know why not. My word's as good as Granbury's any day. But I'll give you the proof you want, and plenty of it."

Trudy kept her eyes fixed on Myers's plump face. It seemed kinder not even to look at Steven.

Chapter Eleven

The evidence was overwhelming. That first interview with Mr. Myers was only the beginning. The evidence of invoices, letters, and interviews seemed only to confirm the weight of guilt. It was hard to believe they'd only begun their research on Monday, and here it was only Thursday and so much information had come in so effortlessly.

Steven had lost his look of charmed youth and went around dejected and tired. And he didn't know the half of it. Most of the information she'd gained, Trudy kept to herself.

Thursday was the lightest day of Trudy's week. She was through with classes by noon and knew she needed to get back to work on her research.

But she didn't want to. She wanted to get away, to escape. But there was no place to go. She was only about half a block from her house when she glanced ahead to see a figure standing on the porch. Her mother was there waiting for her.

She couldn't deal with her mother. Not today. Turning, she walked rapidly away. She didn't want to go back to school and have to face Steven, and she couldn't go home. Maybe she'd run over to the McFarlin Street Church. It was a peaceful, restful place.

Mentally she kicked herself. She didn't want to make any excuses to be near Jeremy. That was all over. It had to be.

In the end she indulged in an inexcusable extravagance by renting a small economy car from a nearby agency and driving out of town. She had to get away and find some kind of perspective on her problems.

She drove aimlessly at first, then realized she was following a familiar road. She glanced at her own face in the car mirror, then shrugged.

She was headed toward another church, the small one where Jeremy had conducted the wedding ceremony of his friend. Oh well, one place was as good as another. This at least offered a remote, beautiful countryside. She would drive and think things through.

But as the miles fell away she found herself growing more and more tangled in her own thoughts. It wasn't fair, just when she was getting what she wanted out of life, when she was getting the excellent training and experience that would hand her the future on a platter, that this should happen. Her mother and Jeremy and the Granburys were complicating everything.

The drive finally ended at midafternoon in front of the little church. No cars were out front today, but this was the sort of day Owen's bride had deserved, sunny and warm, a day bright with joy.

Trudy smiled sourly. The bridal couple that day hadn't needed sunshine to enhance their happiness, while today even the brightest sunlight couldn't make her feel happy.

She got out to stroll across the grounds. They were in a half-wild state, with grass that was ankle deep and trees growing thickly and randomly. The place bore little resemblance to the carefully manicured lawns of the college, and yet Trudy liked it better.

She stooped to pluck a late-blooming flower.

"Hello there!" The unexpected hail brought her abruptly upright. She smiled when she saw it was the elderly pastor of the church.

"Reverend McDonald," she greeted him.

He peered nearsightedly at her through glasses. "I don't believe I know—" He interrupted himself with a shake of his head. "It's Jerry's girl!"

Trudy smiled, restraining herself from telling him that she was a woman, not a girl, and that she most certainly didn't belong to Jeremy Harper. She reminded herself that she would never see Reverend McDonald again, so there was no use upsetting him by trying to make him understand the truth of either situation.

"What are you doing in this neck of the woods? Did Jerry bring you?" He looked around as though expecting to see Harper.

Trudy shook her head. "I needed to get away alone and think things through, and I remembered your lovely part of the state. I hope you don't mind my trespassing."

"Can't trespass here. I always thought a church should be open twenty-four hours a day, though they tell me now in the cities things are getting stolen and smashed up all the time." He shook his head, looking troubled. "Hard for me to imagine anyone doing damage to a church building."

His expression brightened suddenly. "But now, if you don't mind a little company, you could do me a real favor."

Trudy frowned slightly. "What's that?"

"Come back to the house with me and spend some time with Rachel. It's one of her bad days, and it would cheer her considerably to have a visit from Jerry's girl. He was always a particular favorite with her."

Jerry's girl. It had a nice sound to it, the way it would have been if she'd grown up out here and she and Jeremy were both teenagers, dating and thinking about getting married. A kind of innocent, lovely world she'd never known.

"Your wife is ill?" she asked.

"It's her arthritis—she's got the rheumatoid kind. Doctor told us she was fortunate not to get it until she was in her sixties. Months go by and it doesn't bother her, but then again, there's times like these."

"She wouldn't want to bother with me if she's feeling badly," Trudy protested.

"Nonsense. It'd be just the thing. Give her a chance to fill you in on what Jerry was like as a little fellow. That way you'll know what to expect."

Trudy was tempted. She wanted to hear about the little boy Jeremy used to be. The elderly minister looked frail enough to blow away in the wind. Perhaps there was some way she could help a little, perhaps food or do errands for the two of them. "If you think it wouldn't be a bother."

He beamed at her. "Our house is just down the road to the south," he said. "I walked down, but if you'll give me a lift we can get there at the same time."

Rachel McDonald looked ill. Her face was drawn with pain, her eyes shadowed, but she seemed pleased to see Trudy. "I've thought so often about you and Jerry," she said, enfolding Trudy in a maternal but cautious hug.

Trudy felt as though she were masquerading, operating under false credentials. They assumed she and Jeremy were considerably closer than they were.

Mrs. McDonald allowed her to prepare hot tea and then directed her to the canister with the homemade cookies in it. The three of them found comfortable chairs in the little living room to drink their tea and chat. Trudy loved the stories about Jeremy as a little boy, although he sounded a lot like Phil—naughty and able to find trouble even when he wasn't looking for it.

Mrs. McDonald enjoyed talking about the little boy who had been part of their lives, but when the Reverend McDonald started reminiscing it became evident that he was a sports fan. He talked of Jerry's days as a football star, both in college and as a member of a professional team.

"Everybody thought he was crazy when he threw up his chances and went into the ministry." Reverend McDonald shook his head. "But Rachel and I, we understood." He reached out to touch his wife's hand, and she smiled lovingly at him.

"Jerry had been here several times to talk to us," she confided. "He talked about how he seemed to have everything that anybody could want—success, fame, money—but no peace, no real sense of fulfillment."

Trudy was hard put to keep from openly chuckling at their excessive devotion to Jeremy. Still, it wasn't as though they believed, as she once had, that he was some sort of spiritually elevated being because he was a minister. They saw his faults and his struggles . . . and they loved him.

"The Lord can be puzzling." McDonald shook his head. "All that football experience!" He sounded almost regretful, and Trudy gleefully suspected that to James McDonald the choice to pull Jeremy out of professional football was a mystery indeed.

It was time to be getting back. Trudy glanced

around at the homey little cottage, reluctant to leave. Here she could almost believe anything.

Gently, Rachel McDonald put down her cup, a confused look on her face. "My dear," she said. "Have you come to terms with God's role in your life?"

Trudy set her cup down too, terribly embarrassed. "I believe there is a God," she said. "I just lost track of him during my lifetime."

Rachel McDonald turned to her husband. "Don't know why I came out and asked like that. I thought surely Jerry's young woman believed, but it just seemed to come to me."

He patted her hand. "You were led by the Lord."

Trudy got to her feet. The lovely afternoon was spoiled. "You might as well know I'm not Jerry's young woman, or Jerry's anything. We're only friends."

Rachel McDonald shook her head. "I could see the way you looked at each other."

Trudy looked from the silvery-haired woman to the dignified old man. They had to know the truth. "I'm not Jerry's girlfriend, and I'm not the type who'd become a minister's wife," she said firmly.

It was the worst moment of a terrible day. Both her feelings and thoughts were black, and Trudy wondered what in the world she kept fighting through life for. There seemed no purpose at all.

She didn't want to listen anymore, but Reverend McDonald motioned her back into her chair, and she had no wish to hurt the kindly old man.

"It tells in the Bible how a man named Nicodemus, a leader of the people, came to Jesus at night. I guess he didn't want his friends to know what he was doing. He said to Jesus that he believed He'd come from God because nobody could do the miracles He'd done except if God was with Him. I've seen miracles, Trudy, in my own heart. I'd like you to see them too."

Trudy closed her eyes. It would be nice to see life the way Jeremy and this old couple did . . . trusting that no matter how bad things seemed, there was purpose and reason behind everything.

Mrs. McDonald spoke softly. "I like to think of the caterpillar turning into a butterfly," she explained. "Jesus wants each of us to be born into the butterfly He meant us to be, instead of crawling around on the ground all our lives."

Reverend McDonald smiled at his wife. "Rachel has a turn for the poetic," he said. "Sometimes she even gets a mite fanciful."

"I want to believe," Trudy confessed. "I haven't had a solid faith in anything for years. Sometimes I just yearn for the peace I used to feel, and I wonder if I'll ever feel anything like it again."

"Believe," the elderly minister told her gently. "Pray for it. It's not of the mind alone, nor of the feelings, but all of you."

Trudy closed her eyes.

"Let's pray," Reverend McDonald said.

They prayed for her, and then, haltingly, Trudy herself spoke a few words. She didn't know how much longer they prayed, but she opened her eyes to a new world.

Her heart bubbled joy. A new peace and contentment was within her. At that moment, she had no doubts at all. She was on the peak of the highest mountaintop in God's kingdom.

Rachel McDonald quoted softly. " 'Let not your heart be troubled: ye believe in God, believe also in me.' "

Trudy hugged the older woman. "I'll remember that," she said, "though right now I don't feel like my heart will ever be troubled again."

The minister's wife looked uneasy. "I'm glad you feel that way, dear. But remember, life will hold the same struggles for you."

Trudy said her good-byes to the old couple, walking on air into the darkening afternoon. Much of her drive back would be in the night, but that didn't bother her. She could find her way. With God's help, she could find her way through any darkness. She would be a different person from now on. Inwardly she hummed the first line of the passage Mrs. McDonald had quoted. "Let not your heart be troubled. Let not your heart be troubled." The motion of the car seemed to murmur the words.

The lights of the town slightly dimmed her new-found enthusiasm. The jar of coming down from a spiritual mountaintop to the reality of her everyday life flickered through her mind only momentarily.

Everything was going to be different now. She was going to be different. She would take a good look at her problems and would make rational, responsible decisions.

The first thing was to get something to eat. She pulled the rental car into a parking spot next to the student center and went into the cafeteria. She selected her meal and was carrying the food to a table when she was stopped abruptly by the sight of the couple dining in intimate conversation in a far corner of the big room. It was Jeremy and Melissa, their heads bent close together. He was concentrating on her so intently that Trudy knew she didn't have to worry about her presence being discovered.

The intense stab of jealousy kept her rooted on the spot a moment longer; then she shakily found her way to the opposite corner of the dining room behind a large plastic plant, where they would be unable to see her.

She looked down at the suddenly tasteless food on her plate. If she cared this much—so much that she couldn't stand to see his attention toward Melissa without becoming physically ill—then maybe she should do something about it.

She only managed to eat a little of her dinner, then left the cafeteria with one last glance at the little table in the far corner. Jeremy and Melissa were still talking.

She went back to her room. A note was taped on the door. "Urgent. Mrs. Samuels insists you call her."

The number was written beneath the words. This was too much! Trudy tossed the note angrily into the wastebasket. She sank down on her bed. The most she could handle tonight was simply getting ready to go to sleep.

The phone rang. She waited several minutes, not answering, afraid it was her mother. She would just let it ring.

Willpower deserted her and she picked up the receiver. It was neither her mother nor Jeremy, but a little boy's voice that addressed her. "Hi, Trudy," Phil said.

"Hello, Phil," Trudy returned the greeting. "How are you?"

"I'm better. I'm home again."

"I'm sure you're glad."

"Nope. There was lots going on at the hospital. Nurses and doctors always coming by. People coming to visit me. I'm bored."

Trudy couldn't help chuckling. He was lucky to be alive, but a few days later he was bored because nothing exciting was happening. Then the laughter faded. It was like her own story. This afternoon she'd been through an experience that had changed her life . . . and tonight here she was reacting to things in the same old way.

"What can I do to help?" she asked.

"You could come and see me tomorrow," he suggested.

Mentally she flipped through her schedule. "How about the middle of the afternoon? I have a couple of hours free then." She would hang on to the rented car for another day. That way she could see for herself that Phil was all right.

"That'd be great," he responded enthusiastically. "And, Trudy, do you suppose you could bring Mike too?"

Trudy couldn't help laughing. "And here I thought you wanted to see me, and all the time you were only trying to con me into bringing your friend out there."

"I do want to see you," Phil assured her earnestly. "But it'd be twice as nice if Mike could come too."

"I don't even know where he lives," Trudy protested, "or if his parents will let him come."

"He lives in the little green house on the corner where the car hit me. I'll feel so much better if you and Mike come to see me. . . ." His voice trailed off weakly.

"You're not deceiving me, young man," Trudy informed him, "but I will go by and see if Mike can drive out with me."

It wasn't until she hung up that Trudy remembered that Betsy Granbury didn't approve of her son's friendship with Mike and would most likely not welcome him to her home. Oh well, she'd already promised. She'd do her best not to disappoint Phil.

She'd slipped into her pajamas and was preparing to go to bed, determined to shut all of tomorrow's problems out of her head, when the phone rang again.

This time she didn't fool herself that she could

refrain from answering, but she breathed more easily when she recognized Steven's voice on the other end of the line. The relief was short-lived, however.

"Trudy," he said, barely bothering with the preliminaries of a greeting. "I've done more digging today."

She knew immediately it was bad news. He sounded as young as Phil, and disappointed and confused. She wished Dr. Lorimer had never assigned him to this particular story.

"How does it look, Steven?" she asked soberly.

"Bad." His voice was so low she had to strain to hear it. "And I thought if there was anyone I could trust . . ." His voice broke off. When he spoke again he sounded stronger. "I don't believe it. It's got to be some kind of mistake. Dad wouldn't do the things they claim. We've got to prove them wrong."

Trudy didn't know what to say.

Chapter Twelve

The next afternoon when Trudy drove out to Seven Oaks, she not only had Mike at her side, but he held the wiggling black puppy in his lap.

He'd insisted that Phil needed a visit from Blackie. Trudy had little doubt how Phil would welcome the puppy, but she wasn't too sure about his mother.

When they arrived at the luxurious farm, she told the boy to remain outside with the dog while she found out if Phil could see them. If they were to be refused, she didn't want Mike's feelings hurt.

To her surprise, Jeremy answered the door. When he saw who it was, a look of pleasure spread across his rugged face.

"I came to see Phil," she said. "He invited me."

He grinned at her. "The way I heard it, it was more of a command performance."

"You knew about it?" she asked, surprised.

"Sure. He couldn't resist bragging to me that you were coming out when I stopped by for a visit last night. So I managed to persuade him to let me be a party to the occasion." He stepped aside so that she could enter.

Trudy hesitated. She might as well confess all. "It isn't only me," she said. "It's Mike and Blackie."

His eyes danced. "Phil will consider that a real bonanza. How is Mike? I haven't seen him in a day or so."

So he had been keeping up with the boy. "His mother was home from work when I stopped by. She was sick. Nothing serious, just a light case of the flu. She's a nice woman, Jeremy, having a hard time raising that child by herself. She's not a person your sister would disapprove of. She can't help it that she's poor and struggling."

He tilted his head questioningly.

"You said your sister didn't like Phil to play with Mike."

His expression cleared. "That was before I talked to her about it. I had to remind her that our own beginnings were exceedingly humble. Seriously though, what she was concerned about was that Mike was a bad influence on Phil." He grinned again. "I had to explain to her that it was most likely the other way around."

They went out together to bring Mike and

178

Blackie into the house. Jeremy led the way to the back part of the house to a room that was something like a cross between a regular room and a porch. Its walls were mostly glass, opened now to let the soft fall air enter. The furniture was comfortably casual and plants were everywhere, seeming to bring the outdoors inside.

Phil was sprawled on a small sofa, surrounded by his family and looking as bored as he'd tried to convince her he was.

"Look who's here!" his uncle announced.

Betsy Granbury seemed to have resolved to forget her last meeting with Trudy, and the visit passed pleasantly. A light snack was served, after which the group broke up into little conversational clusters. Miles and Betsy Granbury sat a little to one side, chatting quietly together. Trudy found herself seated next to Jeremy. They talked mostly about the two boys, who played noisily with Blackie. Steven sat by himself in a corner, hunched morosely over a book. Trudy didn't have to ask what was bothering him.

Her own thoughtful gaze went to Miles Granbury's face. He was looking lovingly at his pretty wife. Trudy couldn't help shaking her head. If she'd been making a guess, she'd have assumed Granbury a little too idealistic to face the realities of what his life as a senator would be.

It only went to show you couldn't tell by appearances.

"Bored with our simple family life?" Jeremy's caustic question seared across her thoughts.

Startled, she shook her head. "I was only thinking how much I missed growing up without a family of my own."

"We didn't have all these trappings, Betsy and I, but being poor didn't seem to matter much on the farm when Mom and Dad were still there. No one around had much money, so we never felt deprived. It was probably difficult for our parents, never knowing how they would make ends meet. But we were sheltered by them."

She looked thoughtfully at him. Somehow she had associated his brother-in-law's wealth with his own upbringing. So he'd come from a poor family.

"I drove out to your old church yesterday," she said, "and had a visit with the McDonalds."

His expression betrayed surprise, but when he spoke, his voice sounded natural enough. "How were they?"

"Mrs. McDonald was having a bad day with her arthritis, but we had a lovely visit anyway."

Her secret was bursting within her, aching to be told. But words seemed too ordinary. When she spoke, her voice came out a whisper. "I have finally come to terms with my faith and found some peace."

For a second he didn't move, and Trudy was conscious of the boys' jubilant yells, of the soft murmur of conversation from Betsy and Miles. Then he took both her hands in his, squeezing them wordlessly.

Suddenly a bouncing black puppy landed

abruptly in Trudy's lap. Mike raced after him, all apologies, and for no reason at all Trudy found herself laughing.

"So much for life's dramatic moments," she told Jeremy, scratching the puppy's head.

"I'm trying to teach him manners," Mike explained, standing earnestly before them.

"He'll learn if you keep trying," Jeremy assured him. "He's young yet, and it's only natural for him to make mistakes."

"Like our Phil." Miles Granbury came over to arrange the sofa cushion on which his stepson reclined into a more comfortable position. "Though he is learning."

Phil looked up seriously at his stepfather. "I'm going to be lots more careful about cars," he promised. "I won't run into the street again without looking."

"Yeah," his brother interjected cynically. "Next time you'll find a different way to get into trouble."

Trudy laughed with the others, uncomfortably aware that the research she was gathering with her tape recorder and notebook could very well destroy this pleasant family scene. Phil and Steven looked up to this man who had come to fill the role of father in their lives. How would the revelation of his true character change them?

Trudy's gaze went across the room to the blond woman, who was watching her younger son with a fond smile. Jeremy said his sister had been through a lot in her first marriage. How would

181

she handle this blow?

Back at the McDonalds' it had seemed so easy to live the Christian life, but already it was proving to be extremely difficult. Did she have a right to go ahead with her research and write the story that would wither the Granburys' happiness?

And Jeremy . . . would Jeremy hate her? It couldn't matter. She'd already reaffirmed her decision that he should play no part in her life. Trudy McClung could never fill the role of minister's wife.

The night before, when she'd seen him with Melissa in the cafeteria, she should have been pleased that things were working out in that direction. Melissa was typecast for the part of Jeremy's wife. But Trudy was going to have to work quite a while at being happy about it.

Abruptly she got to her feet. "Afraid we'll have to break this up, Mike. I've got to get back to work."

Mike only looked at her reproachfully, but Phil protested out loud. "Stay a little longer, Trudy," he pleaded. "Mike and me only just started playing."

Trudy gestured helplessly. "I'd like to, Phil, but I have an appointment with Dr. Lorimer, and he's my boss."

"How about letting Mike and Blackie stay a little longer anyway?" Jeremy suggested. "I'll take them back later."

It seemed an agreeable compromise, and Trudy

gave in without debate. She hated to interrupt the boys' fun.

"Can I hitch a ride with you?" Steven stirred in his corner. "Uncle Jerry brought me out, so my car's still in town."

Trudy was conscious of Jeremy's half-frowning gaze as he looked at his nephew crossing the room toward her. Jealousy might be an undesirable emotion, but it was obviously being felt by the pastor of the McFarlin Street Church as he watched his handsome young nephew.

She told herself she shouldn't be pleased.

"I couldn't stand it any longer," Steven muttered as they walked to the car together.

Trudy didn't have to ask what he was talking about. "It's my responsibility," she said. "Not yours. It wasn't fair of Dr. Lorimer to give you this assignment, and I'm going to ask him to let you off the hook."

"I can take it," he assured her, sounding younger than his years. "I was only sitting there watching Mom and Dad and Phil and wondering what's going to happen when it all comes out. Only, Trudy, I still can't believe it. Dad's not like that, or if he is, he sure had me fooled."

After she'd left the car at the rental agency, Trudy walked slowly up the hill toward the journalism building. Her intent was to ask again that Steven be relieved of the assignment. Maybe she should make the same request for herself.

She saw immediately that the professor was not in the best of moods. He glared wordlessly as she walked into his office.

"You're five minutes late!"

"Sorry," Trudy apologized, certain she was right on time.

"Students today have no concept of commitment to their professions, no idea of the public good. All they want is what they see as glamour and a way to make a fast buck."

Trudy knew it would do no good to argue. She might as well be direct. "You're reasonably aware of the local political scene."

He gazed warily at her. "Don't see how we got to that subject, but yes, I'd say I was more knowledgeable than most."

"You've already admitted you had a good idea Miles Granbury's name would be brought into this little investigation his son and I are conducting."

"Granbury's the fair-haired boy in local politics. His name was bound to come up."

"Then isn't it cruel to continue to involve Steven?" She returned glare for glare, showing him he could no longer intimidate her.

"Perhaps I saw it as giving the boy a chance to see the matter handled fairly."

Steven himself had mentioned that point. It was a hard one to argue. "I came in here to ask to be taken off the assignment."

"Because you're fond of Steven?"

"Steven and the others," she admitted, her thoughts flashing to Steven's uncle.

Dr. Lorimer leaned his chair back precariously,

184

fire fading from his eyes as he studied her philosophically. "Lots of people would know how to handle that. They'd simply see to it that the information gathered was interpreted favorably to their friends. You're a good writer; you could twist it that way."

"I don't twist news," Trudy retorted indignantly.

He frowned. "That's public money they're claiming Granbury has been playing games with. I may be old-fashioned, but I still feel a good journalist has an obligation to the people."

Trudy dropped into a chair. "I don't want to hurt anyone."

"I don't either." He shook his head.

Finally she looked up at the eccentric old professor. He had the reputation of being moody, difficult, and the best in the business. She'd always thought he had the reputation for excellence because of his ability to teach how to write in words that explained clearly and concisely the happenings of the day, how to research and interview. But suddenly she knew it was more than all those skills. He was giving her lessons in the honor and responsibility of being a journalist.

She got to her feet. "I've got to get to work."

"Still want out of that assignment?"

She nodded, not looking at him. "I want out, but I'll keep going anyway."

"What about young Granbury?" he called after her as she stepped into the hall.

"He already knows the worst possibilities.

Perhaps it's best for him to stick it out the rest of the way."

After her tour of duty was completed on the *Daily,* Trudy summoned Steven to her side. "We're going to try to sew up this story in the next day or two."

He agreed dully. "Might as well," he said with all the enthusiasm of a man anticipating his own execution.

The two of them went over each bit of information again, replaying interviews, rereading notes. Trudy began to write, knowing this was bound to be a big story for the student newspaper to break. She and Steven owed Quinlan their gratitude; the scoop was bound to make their reputations at the same time as it destroyed Steven's stepfather's.

"What gets me is that Mr. Quinlan said these guys paid Dad off to get the contracts, but now they're turning around and testifying against him," Steven commented dejectedly. Too tired to work anymore, he'd gone down to the basement and returned with cold drinks for both of them. Trudy would have preferred something other than the cold soda, but the coffee machine was out of order and she was too exhausted to walk across campus to the student center.

"I suppose it's because your dad is no longer in office," she answered.

"They think he's not in a position to do any more favors. But if I were looking for somebody to do me a good turn, I'd think the man people say is going to be the next senator from this part

186

of the state would be a good bet. Even Mr. Quinlan seemed to think so. Why else did he keep coming out to the house last spring, talking to Dad about how he'd like to get into politics?''

Trudy frowned. "Mel Quinlan is interested in politics?''

Steven shrugged. "He might have only been talking big, but I was there when he told Dad he thought it was the only career for an ambitious man. He said there wasn't anything he'd let stand in his way to get the kind of opportunity Dad had.''

Trudy stared, wondering if Steven had any idea what he was saying. Obviously not. His shoulders drooped and his voice dragged.

"What did your father say?'' she asked, her voice carefully casual.

"About what?'' He frowned at her tiredly, already having lost the thread of the conversation.

Trudy tried to be patient. "When Mr. Quinlan said that about doing anything to be a successful politician, what did your dad tell him?''

"Can't remember.'' The frown was still on Steven's face as he tried to think. "Something about how he'd been lucky, and Quinlan laughed kind of nasty like and said something about Dad being born with a silver spoon in his mouth. But that's not the way it happened, Trudy. He worked hard and he wasn't in it for himself. He wanted to make things better for everybody.'' Steven looked down at the clutter of papers on the desk where they'd been working. "Or at least, that's what I used to think."

Only a few moments before, Trudy had been too tired to think, but now she felt a new excitement flowing through her veins. It was more than the wish to vindicate Miles Granbury and spare his family. It was the good reporter's instinct for truth. Steven's recollections brought a new element into the story.

Thinking she'd better not get the boy's hopes up in case she was wrong, Trudy patted his hand as though he were as young as Phil. "Go on home, Steven," she said. "It's late."

He rubbed at his eyes as though working to keep them open. "I'll drive you over to your place first."

She shook her head. "I have some things to do. Go on home."

He scowled reluctantly, but then a voice spoke from the doorway behind them.

"I'll see her safely home, Steven," Jeremy said.

He waited until his nephew left before addressing her directly. "I've been stalking you all evening. Went by your place, the student center, and even the library. Thought you might be studying there. Then I saw the light in the *Daily* offices and knew who must be burning the midnight oil."

"Midnight?" She looked blearily at her watch. "It can't be that late."

"It's only about eleven," he admitted. "But you'd better leave your big story until tomorrow and get home and get some sleep."

"I have something important to do first." She wished he would go away, but he seemed determined to stay at her side until he'd seen her home as promised. If it was already eleven, she couldn't afford to wait until she got home to make her call. She couldn't bear to wait until morning to know its outcome.

Despite Jeremy's presence, she'd go ahead and call. He couldn't possibly guess what it was about. She picked up the receiver and dialed the number Quinlan had given her as his home phone.

A sleepy-voiced woman answered and seemed annoyed when Trudy asked for Mr. Quinlan.

"My husband's had a long day." The voice sharpened protectively. "Can't you talk to him tomorrow?"

Trudy injected firmness into her tone. "Tell him it's Trudy McClung," she said. "I'm sure he'll speak to me."

She was conscious of Jeremy, strolling to the other side of the room, pretending disinterest. But there was no way he could keep from hearing her side of the conversation.

Mel Quinlan's deep voice boomed at her. "Miss McClung, what can I do to help you?"

"Some new information has come to my attention. I need to see you."

"Tonight? But it's late already."

"It's most significant, Mr. Quinlan," she insisted firmly.

"You've got something new on Granbury!" His

voice was beginning to show interest. "It's about time. I've been wondering when you were going to run that story. You've taken so much time I was about ready to go to another paper."

"Our story will probably be scheduled to run soon," she told him, "but as I said, something new and important has come up and I need to talk to you about it immediately."

"Where can I meet you?"

Trudy looked around. "I'm at the journalism school," she volunteered hesitantly, "but it might be better if I came over to your place."

"He won't like that," Jeremy whispered. "His wife is more than a little jealous, and she wouldn't like a pretty little thing like you visiting her husband."

Trudy covered the mouthpiece with one hand. "You're not supposed to be listening," she reminded him coldly.

"I think it would be better if I met you at the school, Miss McClung. I'll be right there."

She heard a click on the other end before she could protest, and she turned to Jeremy Harper. She had to get rid of him before Quinlan arrived.

Chapter Thirteen

"I'm not leaving," he said before she could even speak. "I need to talk to you. And it's about something important, too."

She hoped he wasn't going to tell her again he loved her. She looked pointedly at her watch. "Mr. Quinlan will be here right away."

"I can talk fast. A woman came by my office this afternoon, a Mrs. Dorothy Samuels. She said she'd learned we were friends."

"Word does get around," Trudy murmured. She simply could not deal with this right now.

"Your mother is worried about you." He cleared a place on her desk and sat down on one edge.

Trudy remained standing. "She only worries about herself," she told him bitterly. "She wants to start a new life for the dozenth time and wants my stamp of approval."

"She told me about that too. But she said the real reason she's still here is because of you. She loves you, Trudy, and wants the bad feelings erased that lie between you."

Trudy laughed, the sound unpleasant in her own ears. "Erased?" She made a motion as though moving an eraser across a blackboard. "Just like that. All the bad things she's ever done wiped out like they'd never happened."

He reached out to put his arms around her, pulling her to him.

"I want to forgive her," she continued. "It hurts me as much as her that I go on hating, but getting my life in order hasn't automatically made me able . . ."

She stopped, irritated at the way he was smiling at her. "She was always good at saying things. Obviously she's convinced you. But you'll have to learn there's more to truth than what people tell you." Bitterly she made a sudden decision. "Stay here until Mr. Quinlan comes; then maybe you'll get a good lesson about the way people really are."

She regretted the challenge the minute she'd spoken it, but he moved back to look at her questioningly, and before she could withdraw it, Mel Quinlan walked into the room.

"Thought I might have trouble locating you," he said, "but the *Daily* office was lighted—" He broke off to frown at the minister.

"What's he doing here?" He growled the question at Trudy, inclining his head in Harper's direction. "Beg pardon, Reverend, but this is a private matter."

"It won't be a private matter after the story comes out in the *Daily*," she reminded him. "It'll be picked up by papers all over the state."

"Still, his sister's married to Granbury."

"Mr. Quinlan, I have every intention of disclosing the information we've obtained to Mr. Granbury before publication. He has a right to have his side reported as well. So what can it matter that Dr. Harper hears about it a little in advance?"

Quinlan nodded reluctantly. Trudy almost expected some sort of question from Jeremy, but he stood formally at her side. Trudy decided she would be less at a disadvantage with the two men if she got them to sit down.

She pulled a couple of chairs up by her desk and sat down in her own chair. Quinlan and Jeremy also sat, but eyed each other suspiciously.

"You might as well know, Reverend, we've got some real solid proof that your brother-in-law has had his hand in the public till."

"Nonsense!" Jeremy sounded amused.

"Unfortunately it seems to be true, Jerry," she said, using the name his family called him. "Mr. Quinlan and some others claim bribes were paid to Mr. Granbury while he was county commissioner."

"They only went along with the bribing as evidence," Quinlan hastily assured Jeremy.

"They were involved in this 'evidence' over a period of several years according to the material I have," Trudy observed, allowing a note of skepticism to enter her voice.

Jeremy shook his head. "Sometimes I've thought Miles was letting himself in for some bad shocks, getting deeper into politics. He might be deceived by his trust in others, but to deliberately defraud the public? Never."

"We've got the evidence," Quinlan said, looking at Trudy for confirmation. "Solid evidence." He seemed a little nervous.

"The evidence does seem solid," Trudy admitted. "But I let myself get personally involved in this story. That's the only excuse I have for letting my judgment get so clouded."

Quinlan frowned at her. "Look, Miss McClung, if you're saying you're so fond of that Granbury boy who's been helping you with the work that you won't go after his old man, then there are plenty of other reporters who will be glad to get this story."

"I'm sure they would," Trudy admitted. "And if you look long enough, you'll probably even find one or two careless enough to do the bad research job I've done."

"Bad research?" He looked at her suspiciously as though trying to figure out what she was getting at.

Trudy looked down at her desk. "Something Steven said tonight made me think. He said you envied his father his political career, that you wanted to go into politics yourself."

"Quinlan ran for commissioner against Miles that first term," Jeremy contributed. "But that was back when I was still in college and not even acquainted with Miles, so I don't know much about it."

"I lost," Quinlan admitted. "Didn't have the Granbury money to finance my campaign."

Jeremy spoke again. "You've done all right," he said. "Quinlan Motors and your various other enterprises are booming."

"That's right." Quinlan nodded. "It's time for me to make another try."

"Perhaps you were thinking of running for state senate, Mr. Quinlan." Trudy's voice was smooth as silk. "But there is one large obstacle. Miles Granbury is well thought of in this area. Everyone says he's sure to win."

She was barely conscious of Jeremy's continued presence. Her attention was concentrated on Quinlan's face. He was beginning to perspire.

"I've got solid evidence," he said again.

Trudy shook her head. "It suddenly occurred to me, Mr. Quinlan, that you've supplied all the information—the documents, the invoices, everything. Papers can be faked, Mr. Quinlan, but experts can tell. Is that why you came to a student newspaper? Was it because you didn't want a top-rate professional on the job? You wanted the story printed, and once it was, the slur would probably never be erased from Granbury's name."

He mopped his face with a handkerchief. "That's ridiculous. You talked to Myers and the others."

"Your friends, Mr. Quinlan. The interviews were arranged by you. I really must apologize."

"Apologize?" He was looking confused at this unexpected turn of events. "What are you talking about?"

Trudy got to her feet. "I'm usually a good reporter. I don't let other people do my legwork for me. I do my own checking, talk to sources I dig out for myself. But you seemed to have this all set up for me, Mr. Quinlan. That's what it was, wasn't it? A setup. You were going to frame Miles Granbury."

Quinlan stuttered his protest, but when neither of them responded, he looked down. "Granbury deserves to take a fall. Thinks he's so high and mighty."

Trudy spoke in a low voice. "I think you'd better go, Mr. Quinlan. I'm going to have to start all over again and dig until I find the story that's really there."

To her surprise, he straightened up and managed a grudging smile. "Maybe you'd better let it rest," he said, "but it was a good try. It almost worked."

She watched in amazement as he left the room, listening to his footsteps echoing along the hall. "Can you believe that man?"

Jeremy nodded soberly. "I can," he said. "But

Miles is going to shocked. He thinks they're friends.''

Trudy walked over to where he was still seated. She was tired, but she felt as good as though she'd just completed a terrific story. She laughed. ''I threw away a story that could have made my career, and I'm delighted. Isn't that crazy? I don't know what's going on.''

She looked down at him and resisted a mad impulse to smooth his hair with her hand. ''I don't know what will happen to me now. I've always lived for my ambition.''

''The ambition's still there,'' he told her. ''But in proper proportion. And you have other things in your life as well now.''

''Like what?''

He stood up, folding his arms loosely around her so she stood within his grasp, but he could still look into her face. ''Like me,'' he answered simply.

She avoided his eyes. ''I thought I would be different after yesterday, but I'm still the same person with the same problems, making the same old mistakes.'' She waited for his comment, but then she knew the answer without being told. ''I am different, but that doesn't mean everything's going to be easy and I'm never going to make mistakes or get mad or . . .''

She stopped. The time had come when she would have to tell him to go away in a manner that left no doubt of her sincerity. But it felt so good having him close, being held in his arms.

"One thing I've learned. People can change. I have. It's because of that . . . that I have no choice but to give my mother another chance to be different too. It's not that I'm gullible, Jeremy. She's failed me too many times."

Trudy closed her eyes, trying to think how to explain. "I've grown up enough to risk giving her another chance."

She had a sudden image of what it would be like, of the trembling happiness in her mother's face, of the way she would want to hold Trudy against her as though she were still a little girl.

It would be a risk because, grown up or not, she still wanted a close relationship with her mother. But now there was a second, more important need—for another person.

She tried to push him away. "I'm so tired I'm giddy," she said, "or I wouldn't let you hold me like this."

"I like it," he murmured contentedly. "It's nice."

"Nice!" she commented indignantly. "It's supposed to be exciting and world-shaking, not just nice."

His lips were warm against hers, and she allowed herself to be lost in the moment. Somewhere in the back of her mind she excused the weakness by telling herself she was only taking advantage of this one last opportunity. Only she'd used that excuse before.

She pulled away abruptly.

"Trudy, I love you," he protested. "If you'll only agree to marry me, I'll give you all the time you need to adjust to the idea."

"I don't need time," Trudy answered confusedly. "I know already." She stopped. She'd been about to say she loved him and would marry him as soon as possible. "You're the minister. Who would marry us?"

"Jim McDonald might be persuaded to perform that function," he assured her, his face suddenly glowing, and she knew he was assuming her answer meant yes. "Both he and Rachel would be so pleased."

"They think I'm the one for you," Trudy said, not understanding why she was rambling on this way. Why didn't she come right out and make it clear she had no intention of marrying him? "They said they could tell by the way we looked at each other."

He tried to draw her into his embrace again, but she resisted. "It's Melissa you should marry," she told him, feeling miserable, as though she were speaking her own death sentence.

"Melissa?" He stared as though having trouble following the conversation. Trudy knew they had no business discussing anything so important to both their lives when they'd both been through so much already this evening. They were liable to say things they didn't mean, make promises neither could keep.

"Melissa." She said the name again. "Your sister was right; she'd be perfect for you. If I were a movie director casting the role, I'd choose Melissa.''

He laughed. ''I told you I don't love Melissa. I've tried to avoid hurting her feelings, but last night I finally had to sit her down and make her listen.'' His mouth twisted wryly. ''Trudy, I think she was more angry than hurt.''

''But, Jeremy, you shouldn't burn your bridges,'' Trudy protested. ''You do need a wife. You need someone to confide in, someone to understand what you go through in your work.''

''Everyone needs someone to love and share things with.'' He smoothed her hair, touched one ear with a gentle fingertip. Trudy shivered deliciously.

''I love you,'' he said again. ''And now that Melissa is out of the picture, you'll have to marry me or I'll be alone for the rest of my life. It was when I told Betsy how I felt about you that she came around. She said if I was that sure . . .''

''You're really sure?'' Trudy asked wistfully, wanting to be convinced it could work.

''That I love you? No doubts,'' he promised. ''None at all.''

''But what about your work? How would I fit into that? I'd say awful things, and people would think I was all wrong to be your wife.''

''Darling,'' he said, holding her once again. ''Don't you think I've wondered how I would fit into your world? It goes two ways. But I've prayed most seriously, knowing there was a time when what I thought I wanted and what God

200

wanted for me were two different things."

"You prayed about us?"

"I prayed, and I'm still here. That's your answer," he assured her. He released her, going over to stand on the other side of the office as though telling her the decision wasn't entirely an emotional one, influenced by the heady presence of the woman he loved in his arms.

"This isn't a movie, my love," he said. "I'm not looking for someone who will speak and look and always act in a particular way. The qualities you have are the ones God meant you to have. I've never known anyone kinder or more perceptive. Look how you are with Mike and his mother, with Phil . . ."

She understood what he was telling her. She wanted so much to believe him. She looked at him, the tall strong man who would be her husband. Her heart seemed to be overflowing. It took only a moment for her to close the gap that existed between them.

The publishers hope that this Large Print Book has brought you pleasurable reading. Each title is designed to make the text as easy to see as possible. G. K. Hall Large Print Books are available from your library and your local bookstore. Or you can receive information on upcoming and current Large Print Books and order directly from the publisher. Just send your name and address to:

G. K. Hall & Co.
70 Lincoln Street
Boston, Mass. 02111

or call, toll-free:

1-800-343-2806

A note on the text
Large Print edition designed by
Bernadette Strickland.
Composed in 16 pt English Times
on an Editwriter 7700
by Debra Nelson of G. K. Hall Corp.